"*I want you to marry me.*"

Indecision tore at her. Tears she had refused to shed for herself clustered behind her eyes, for him. There was really only one consideration that mattered—he was Genie's father, facing the worst crisis anyone could have to face. For Genie's sake she knew what her answer must be. "Yes, I'll marry you, James."

His hand shot out and a crooked finger caught a single tear as it slid down her cheek. "I hope these are not for me, Zoe. They would only complicate things."

She frowned. "What do you mean?"

"You mustn't make the mistake of caring about me. Only the thought that you're doing this for Genevieve will make it work." He smiled tiredly, the humor failing to reach his eyes. "You may think me heartless, but I'm not so unfeeling as to want to leave behind a grieving widow."

Dear Reader,

To ring in 1998—Romance-style!—we've got some new voices and some exciting new love stories from the authors you love.

Valerie Parv is best known for her Harlequin Romance and Presents novels, but *The Billionaire's Baby Chase,* this month's compelling FABULOUS FATHERS title, marks her commanding return to Silhouette! This billionaire daddy is *pure* alpha male...and no one—not even the heroine!—will keep him from his long-lost daughter....

Doreen Roberts's sparkling new title, *In Love with the Boss,* features the classic boss/secretary theme. Discover how a no-nonsense temp catches the eye—and heart—of her wealthy brooding boss. If you want to laugh out loud, don't miss Terry Essig's *What the Nursery Needs...* In this charming story, what the *heroine* needs is the right man to make a baby! Hmm...

A disillusioned rancher finds himself thinking, *Say You'll Stay and Marry Me,* when he falls for the beautiful wanderer who is stranded on his ranch in this emotional tale by Patti Standard. And, believe me, if you think *The Bride, the Trucker and the Great Escape* sounds fun, just wait till you read this engaging romantic adventure by Suzanne McMinn. And in *The Sheriff with the Wyoming-Size Heart* by Kathy Jacobson, emotions run high as a small-town lawman and a woman with secrets try to give romance a chance....

And there's *much* more to come in 1998! I hope you enjoy our selections this month—and every month.

Happy New Year!

Joan Marlow Golan
Senior Editor
Silhouette Books

Please address questions and book requests to:
Silhouette Reader Service
U.S.: 3010 Walden Ave., P.O. Box 1325, Buffalo, NY 14269
Canadian: P.O. Box 609, Fort Erie, Ont. L2A 5X3

THE BILLIONAIRE'S BABY CHASE

Valerie Parv

Silhouette

ROMANCE™

Published by Silhouette Books

America's Publisher of Contemporary Romance

For Margie and Tony, my favorite parent role models

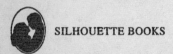 SILHOUETTE BOOKS

ISBN 0-373-19270-3

THE BILLIONAIRE'S BABY CHASE

Printed in U.S.A.

Books by Valerie Parv

Silhouette Romance

The Leopard Tree #507
The Billionaire's Baby Chase #1270

VALERIE PARV

lives and breathes romance and has even written a guide to being romantic, crediting her cartoonist husband of twenty-six years as her inspiration. As a former buffalo and crocodile hunter in Australia's Northern Territory, he's ready-made hero material, she says.

When not writing her novels and nonfiction books, or speaking about romance on Australian radio and television, Valerie enjoys dollhouses, being a Star Trek fan and playing with food (in cooking, that is.) Valerie agrees with actor Nichelle Nichols, who said, "The difference between fantasy and fact is that the fantasy simply hasn't happened yet."

Dear Genevieve,

One day you'll be old enough to ask where I was during those early months of your life after you were taken away from me. I want you to know that you were never out of my thoughts. Every time I saw a little girl around the right age, it tore me up inside. I never stopped looking for you or gave up hope of finding you.

When I finally did, my first sight of you gave me that lump-in-the-throat feeling you get when you see a perfect sunset, or hear "Silent Night" playing. Then your tiny hand crept into mine, and the waiting was over.

Thanks to Zoe, who took such good care of you while we were apart, I've heard about the milestones in your small life. I only pray I can share the big ones still ahead of you. If something should happen to me, you'll always have Zoe and the certainty that I loved you enough to find you and bring you home. Always remember you mean the world to me.

Love,

Dad

Prologue

Bill Margolin gave a sigh of frustration but he should have known it would have no effect on his patient who kept his back turned and his gaze on the spectacular view of the Sydney Harbor beyond the plate-glass window.

It was a shame all his patients didn't keep themselves in such great shape, the doctor thought, watching the tall man shrug into his shirt. With what James was facing, he'd need every bit of his strength if he was to survive. Bill hated to be the bearer of bad news, but as a doctor as well as a friend he had to make James understand the risk he was taking.

A wry smile tugged at Bill's mouth. When had anyone ever made James Langford do anything? The man was the original immovable object, a goal-seeking missile who went over or around obstacles if he could, but through them if he had to. But generally they were business obstacles. There was no way he could go around this particular problem and it was Bill's job to convince him.

With another sigh he returned his attention to the X rays

clipped to a lighted board in front of him. When they were students together there had been times when Bill would have killed to have a physique like his friend, to say nothing of James's fabled charm with women—but now wasn't one of those times. "You can't put the operation off much longer," he repeated in his most authoritative doctor-voice.

With decisive movements, James finished dressing then skewered his friend with a look of such blue-eyed intensity that it wasn't hard to see why women flocked around him. James had a knack of giving you his full attention, which made you feel as if you were the most important person in the world at that moment.

James swung a chair around and straddled it, his fingers drumming a tattoo on the back. "You said the bullet hasn't moved since my last scan."

"It hasn't, but that doesn't mean it won't. It's already pressing against a nerve in your spine, which is why you're getting these blinding headaches."

James gave him a rueful glance, massaging his left arm as if the memory was lodged there. "And the tingling and numbness in my arm. No need to remind me."

"If I don't, you'll keep putting off the operation until you keel over for good."

James frowned. "After I got shot by that Middle Eastern fanatic who objected to foreigners working in his country, the doctors assured me operating to remove the bullet would do more harm than good."

"But that was before it started to move. We've been over this already, James. Surgery is your only option. I wish there was another way but there isn't. You have to let me schedule the operation."

"So you can kill me a lot sooner?" It was unfair taking this out on Bill, but right now he was the only target James had. All he needed was another three months, then the doctor could do what he had to and the outcome wouldn't matter so much.

"So you can have a fighting chance to live." The doctor ground out the words. "I know the operation is risky, but leaving the bullet alone until it paralyzes or kills you is a whole lot riskier."

James flattened both palms against his friend's desk and met his concerned gaze squarely. "The bottom line, Bill. Will three months make that much difference?"

Anger flared in the doctor's expression. "You want me to quote you the odds on your survival? I'm a doctor, not a mathematician. I can't encourage you to risk your life so you can complete some business deal."

James's full mouth tightened into a grim line. "You know me better than that, Bill. This isn't about business."

"Then what's so damned urgent it can't wait until you have the surgery?"

"My daughter's future." He leaned over, reveling in the shock on his friend's craggy face, a mirror of his own expression when he'd heard the news earlier today. "The investigators think they've located Genevieve, Bill."

The doctor cleared his throat noisily, a sure cover for an incipient emotional outburst. "Are you sure? After eighteen months, I thought you'd given up hope of finding her."

He should have known that giving up wasn't in James's vocabulary, either. "Not a chance. As soon as you told me I needed the operation, and the risk it entailed, I had the investigators step up their efforts. I have no intentions of dying on that operating table of yours without seeing my daughter again, and installing her in her rightful place as my heir."

He didn't add *if it's the last thing I do,* because they both knew it could be. No point in laboring the obvious, James thought. Bill nodded slowly. "I see why you need your three months."

"Do I have them?"

The doctor ran wiry fingers through his hair, which had been graying since they were at university together. "It's a hell of a risk. I'd want to monitor your condition closely, and you'd need to guarantee to take things as easy as possible."

"Done and done," James assured him. "Thanks, Bill."

The doctor shook his head. "Don't thank me. I probably need my head examined for letting you walk out of here without a firm date for surgery, but I know what it's been like for you since Ruth disappeared with the baby. Where did you locate them finally?"

"Right here in Sydney. They were practically under my nose the whole time and I never knew it," James said grimly.

"Does Ruth know you're on to her?"

A shadow darkened James's features. "Ruth's dead. Sailing accident in the harbor."

Bill didn't waste his breath on platitudes. Any love his friend had known for his wife had been extinguished the day she ran away with their child. After working in the security business in the Middle East where she and James met, Ruth had known how to cover her tracks well. Only a handful of close friends, Bill among them, knew what hell James had endured because of Ruth. He hardly dared to ask, "What about your daughter?"

James reached into his briefcase and pulled out a folder, opening it on the doctor's desk. "I got this two hours ago." On top lay a black-and-white photograph, the edges slightly blurred as if it had been taken covertly from some distance away, which was probably the case. "This woman was taking care of Genevieve for Ruth when she died. The P.I. is certain the child with her is my daughter." His voice dipped huskily as he shoved the photo across the desk.

Bill studied the picture. It showed a tiny girl about four

or five years old astride a pony at the beach. The child's delight fairly leapt off the page at him. At the pony's head stood an equally compelling-looking woman. About five foot six, the doctor estimated, and ideally proportioned for her height. The only excessive thing about her seemed to be the mass of curls tumbling to her shoulders.

Margolin found himself smiling involuntarily as the woman's sunlit pleasure communicated itself to him through the grainy photograph. She looked windblown but happy, her heart-shaped face mirroring the child's pleasure. All her attention was focused on the child astride the pony, as if nothing else mattered in the world. As a father himself, the doctor knew how that felt.

He glanced at James in concern. His friend's eyes were fixed on the photo, the hunger in them almost palpable. "What are you going to do?" Bill asked quietly, feeling his chest tighten. If this turned out to be another false lead, it was going to hit James hard.

His friend dragged his eyes away from the picture as if the effort cost him a great deal. The look he turned on Bill burned with purpose. "By the time I get back to my office, I'll have absolute confirmation that she's my daughter. Then I want to see her, find out how she's been living since she was taken away. This woman, Zoe Holden, apparently fostered her when her family couldn't be traced."

"So she doesn't know who the child belongs to?" A sigh gusted past Bill's lips as James shook his head. "This will come as quite a shock to her."

James's hands balled into fists before he made an obvious effort to relax them. "I'm well aware of how it's going to feel. I've been there, remember?"

"Maybe you should let the authorities handle the initial approach," Bill suggested, knowing it was futile as soon as James flashed him a fierce look.

"If I'd left this to the authorities, I'd still be waiting," he said. "This time I'll handle it my way." He flicked the folder closed. "Zoe Holden is a property manager with a local real estate agency. As it happens, my firm has been looking for somewhere to house executives visiting from overseas and her agency has been advertising a suitable place. I've arranged to inspect the property. It will give me the perfect opportunity to find out what this Zoe Holden is like and what sort of home she's been providing for Genevieve."

Bill whistled soundlessly. "Sounds a bit cloak-and-dagger to me, but it's one way to check her out without tipping your hand. When will you see her?"

James consulted the gold Rolex gleaming on his tanned wrist. "I have an appointment with her this afternoon. As you've spent the morning drumming into me, I don't have the luxury of time to waste. The sooner I get my daughter back, the sooner you can operate. Do we have a deal?"

The doctor frowned. "You can't bargain with your health, but if you follow my orders and take things easy, maybe you can postpone the operation a little longer. Lord knows, you're stubborn enough. And if there is a chance of getting Genevieve back, I can't stand in your way. Now get out of here. I have sick people waiting who are willing to let me help them."

In spite of a lingering headache courtesy of the doctor's poking and prodding, James managed to whistle as he strode through the waiting rooms and headed for the elevator that would deliver him to the underground car park.

Back in his car again he reached for the photo supplied by the private investigator. He must have studied it a hundred times since it was delivered until every detail was burned into his memory, but he still hadn't tired of it. After eighteen months of enduring a wrenching sense of loss every time he set eyes on a four-year-old, he was entitled to feel elated at the sight of this particular child. From her huge dark eyes to a smile that could light up a room by itself, everything about her screamed a rightness he could feel deep inside. This was his daughter. He knew it.

But this time he found his eyes drawn to the woman holding the pony and a different kind of awareness clawed through him, astonishing him with its power and unexpectedness. She was beautiful. Not the kind of beauty you saw on magazine covers, but rather more natural, with a vibrancy that invited attention. Unaware she was being photographed, she looked relaxed and happy, dressed for the beach in figure-hugging shorts and a skimpy T-shirt. James had a momentary vision of himself clasping her around that incredibly slender waist and whirling her around into the air, just to find out if her laugh was as silvery as her smile promised.

Nerves leapt along his spine, aggravating the tender spot where the bullet was lodged in the side of his neck and the jolt of pain brought him back to reality. He took deep, steadying breaths until the pain passed, telling himself all the while that his reaction to the woman was a result of seeing her with his child. That was all it was and all it could ever be. Because once she found out who he was and what he wanted she would sooner cut out his heart than waste a smile on James Langford.

Chapter One

The child planted tiny fists on small hips. "Mummy, what's a spitting image?"

Zoe looked up from the property brief she was studying and suppressed a smile. "It means a person who looks very much like somebody else. Where did you hear that?"

Genie frowned. "Simon's mummy says he's the spitting image of his daddy." She paused, wrinkling her face in concentration. "Am I the spitting image of you?"

Zoe fought to keep her feelings from registering on her face. Genie was far from being her spitting image. The child was as dark as she herself was fair. Genie's eyes, fixed expectantly on her, were a vivid blue in contrast to her own eyes, which were the color of autumn leaves.

A heart-wrenching rush of love for those self-same features tore through Zoe, making her eyes blur with tears of happiness and gratitude. She was blessed to have the chance to be a mother to a child as beautiful both in looks and nature as Genie. They didn't have to look alike to share a bond she could feel like a steel filament stretching between them.

To cover the torrent of emotions flooding through her, she ruffled Genie's thick chestnut hair, so unlike her own tangle of straw-colored curls. "You don't need to be anyone's spitting image, sweetheart. You're a beautiful, precious one-of-a-kind."

Genie sighed heavily. "I don't want a mummy who went away. I want to be borned your little girl so I could be your spitting image."

Zoe felt another jolt deep inside her even as she masked the reaction with a loving smile. Genie so seldom mentioned her real mother that it came as a shock to be reminded of the reality.

She was annoyed with herself for reacting badly to the reminder now, instead of counting her blessings. A child was one blessing her ill-fated marriage to Andrew hadn't bestowed, although she had dreamed of it long and hard enough. There was nothing physically wrong, doctor after doctor had assured her, not unless you counted deep unhappiness. But Andrew's jealous behavior had frozen something deep inside her.

Her life had settled onto a much more even keel since her husband died, although she still shuddered to think of how quickly everything had changed. He simply hadn't believed she was attending a business seminar with a workmate. Convinced she was on her way to meet a man, Andrew had followed her, slamming his car into a telegraph pole in his unseeing rage. He had died instantly.

Zoe no longer allowed herself to dream of an ideal relationship, although the longing for a child of her own was harder to subdue. That she hadn't even been close to managing it had become obvious the day she got the chance to foster Genie and love her as her own. No child could have been more cherished.

Zoe set the folder aside and took Genie's chubby hands in her own. "Don't I tell you almost every day that you are my little girl in every way that matters and I love you very, very much?" The child nodded solemnly and Zoe pulled in a deep breath. "Do you remember the teddy bear I made for your last birthday?"

Genie nodded again. "Yes."

"And Big Ted that Santa brought you before that?"

"When I was little," Genie confirmed so seriously that Zoe had to make an effort not to laugh.

"Do you love Big Ted any less because I didn't make him for you?"

Genie looked affronted at the very idea. "'Course not. I love both my teddies zackly the same."

Zoe enveloped the child in a hug, feeling her eyes threatening to brim again. "Now you know how I feel about you. You're my special little girl and it doesn't matter one bit that you didn't grow inside me."

"Or if Santa brought me." Genie finished on a triumphant note. Then she added more hopefully, "Maybe if I asked Santa—"

"Santa doesn't bring children," Zoe interjected before Genie could embellish the notion. "Any more than he brought you."

Genie chewed her lower lip. "I know, but it would be fun if he could bring me a baby brother or sister."

A pang gripped Zoe. She knew just how Genie felt. Maybe she was getting greedy, but sometimes her arms ached to hold a baby and feel its mouth nuzzling against her breast. The desire for another child to grow with Genie, to share her games and discoveries, and the outpouring of maternal love Zoe knew she had to offer was almost more than she could bear. Not for the first time she made herself count her blessings. She had Genie to love and care for, and it was more than she had ever dreamed would be hers. She managed a tremulous smile. "Speaking of fun, isn't it time you got ready to go to playgroup?"

To Zoe's intense relief, the distraction worked as it usually did. "Are you coming, too?" Genie demanded, all thoughts of Santa and babies miraculously forgotten.

Zoe wished she could distract herself so easily. She shook her head. "Simon's mummy is taking you both today." Simon's mother, Julie, lived next door and was Zoe's friend and self-appointed morale officer. "I have to show a house to a nice man who's coming all the way from the country to see it."

Genie made a face. "Do you have to? Why can't he look at a house by his own self?"

Zoe laughed at the child's persistence. "Because he can't, that's why. Now scoot. Auntie Julie will be here any minute."

The child scampered off down the hall to her bedroom. In minutes she was back, carrying her koala backpack and favorite Barbie doll, just as the doorbell pealed. As soon as Zoe opened it, Genie launched herself at Simon and his mother, who were waiting outside. Amid promises to be good and hugs all around, they left in a flurry of chatter and excitement.

Zoe barely had time to assemble the documents she would need for the house inspection when the doorbell pealed again.

James Langford waited with barely leashed impatience. When he had asked his secretary to arrange the appointment with Zoe Holden, he had not expected to meet her at what was obviously her own home. He had been fully prepared to spin some tale that would end in her inviting him home after they had inspected the Strathfield mansion.

Being invited here was beyond all his expectations and he could barely suppress a shiver of anticipation. He was so close to finding his daughter he could practically taste his success.

The signs of a child in residence made him catch his breath, his chest tightening painfully. A battered tricycle lay on its side on the front lawn while a ball made a splash of scarlet beneath a rosemary bush. In the report which had awaited him on his desk after he returned from the doctor's office the investigators had noted these signs and more.

A good deal more.

The child living with Zoe Holden was unquestionably Genevieve Langford.

It had taken James half an hour before he recovered sufficiently to read beyond that simple statement to the proof the investigators had amassed, and the background they had supplied on the Holden woman.

It seemed she hadn't always worked as a property manager. Until she obtained her real estate agent's license, she'd been a live-in nanny. Her late husband had lived next door to her employer, which was how they'd met. After the husband died, she'd supported herself by looking after other people's children in her home, while she studied for her present career.

According to the report, Ruth had left their child with Zoe frequently while she made a new life for herself under a false name. Thinking of what sort of life she'd chosen, James felt his features tighten. Freed of the constraints of their marriage, she had thrown herself into all sorts of wild adventures, trying everything from parachuting to white-water rafting and, finally, to sailing on Sydney Harbor. She hadn't survived her last escapade.

James's jaw muscles worked as he considered what could have driven his wife to do such crazy things. Was she trying to prove something to herself? Or was she thumbing her nose at James himself, knowing he would never approve of her life-style?

Damn it, he wasn't a tyrant, expecting his wife to sit at home and be a meek little wife and mother. But he did believe that parenthood conveyed some responsibilities, not least of which was surviving to see your child grow to adulthood.

He dragged in a strangled breath. Even though it had happened eighteen months before, finding out about Ruth's death so abruptly had hit him harder than he had expected. Not because he still loved her. He wasn't that much of a fool. But because her death had been so senseless. Like the proverbial candle in the wind, she had burned herself out long before her time. And because she had never discussed her feelings with him, he had no idea what part he himself might have played in the tragedy.

By hiding herself and Genevieve under a false identity, Ruth had left the authorities no way to trace him after her death. According to the investigator's report, all avenues of inquiry had been tried, many of them by Zoe Holden herself. When any family had proved impossible to trace, she had finally fostered the little girl.

There was no doubt that his search was almost over, but he couldn't let himself accept it. Not yet. Until he was reunited with Genevieve, he was reluctant to trust any amount of evidence. But he would trust his instincts. They had urged him to follow just one more hopeless lead and not to give up. Thank providence he hadn't, or he wouldn't be standing here now with his throat drying and his palms sweating while his heart raced a mile a minute. Setting up a modern telecommunications network for a volatile Middle Eastern country hadn't reduced him to this state.

Drawing in a steadying breath, he let his hand edge toward the doorbell again. Before he could press it, the door swung open and he was confronted by the woman whose face he had been studying in photographs all day.

The first thing he realized was that she was more attractive by far than the grainy picture had suggested. She was slighter, too, and as he had suspected, he could have spanned her waist with both hands. What the photo hadn't revealed was the determined lift to her chin and the flash of challenge in her amber eyes which made him feel as if he'd been king-hit. The crackle of awareness arced through him again, stronger now that she was before him in the flesh. It was even more of an effort to gain control of his vocal cords. Only years of top-level business negotiations gave him the skills to conceal her effect on him. "Zoe Holden?" he made himself ask, although he already knew the answer.

She swallowed hard, looked away and then back at him. Could he possibly be having a similar effect on her? To her credit, she sounded composed when she said, "You must be James Langford."

The woman's eyes had widened at the sight of him and although he was used to the reaction, he felt a perverse satisfaction at knowing he had impressed her. He knew his six-foot-two height could be intimidating. His sister accused him of working out deliberately to pack solid muscle around nature's formidable packaging. She was wrong, of course. These days fitness was a business asset. If it made his rivals think twice about crossing him, it was an added bonus.

Intimidated or not, the woman extended her hand and James felt a quick flaring of respect for her. Although her hand was swamped by his larger one, her grip was firm and businesslike. "I'm Zoe, pleased to meet you."

The musical cadence of her voice was as startling as her handshake, although not quite as startling as the mass of golden curls, which crowned an almost classically sculptured head and neck. She was beautiful enough to take a man's breath away. If he had been no more than a client she was to show over a house, he would have been seriously tempted to invite her to discuss the deal with him over dinner that night.

He *was* seriously tempted, he admitted to himself, but was stopped by the certainty that she would want nothing further to do with him once she knew the real reason he was here. "Call me James," he said and she nodded.

She opened the door wider. "Fine, James. I'll get the paperwork for the Strathfield house and we can be on our way."

James waited at the door while Zoe gathered the papers together and slid them into a leather document case. She was aware of his dark eyes following her movements. The attention had an odd, uplifting effect on her mood.

Most of her clients were elderly investors who treated her like a daughter, sometimes inviting her to their family gatherings. It wasn't often she dealt with a man of the caliber of James Langford. She knew him by reputation, of course, as most people did. His company had pioneered satellite communications in Australia and now operated all over the world. He presided over a pay-television network, radio stations and something to do with computer software. The office had supplied her with some background details on him as soon as he showed an interest in the Strathfield mansion.

However, no amount of research could prepare her for the sheer physical impact he had on her. It wasn't only his size, although it was daunting to discover that she only reached his shoulder even in high heels. His eyes were an arresting blue which would have given Paul Newman tough competition.

Coming on top of a long, lean body which had serious athlete written all over it, the effect was thoroughly arresting. But it was more than his appearance that made her catch her breath. He projected a sense of elemental power that was almost mesmerizing. It wasn't hard to see why he was so successful. His air of command had struck her like a physical force as soon as she opened the door. Yet he bore the mantle of power so easily she had the sense that his genes must go all the way back to Alexander the Great in an unbroken line.

She almost laughed aloud at herself. After her disastrous marriage, what did she know about men and their genes? Alexander the Great, indeed. The man was a client. A rich, successful, incredibly virile and attractive one, but still a client. She had no business constructing an entire fantasy around a greeting and a handshake.

Her friend Julie was probably right. She *was* spending too much time either on her own or with Genie. Maybe she should make the effort to circulate more. If she allowed the memory of her marriage to Andrew to sour the rest of her life, she would let him defeat her twice.

Circulating was one thing, she knew. Allowing herself to get involved with a man, especially a take-charge man like James Langford, was quite another. Nobody knew better than Zoe that getting involved meant giving up control of your life. In Andrew's case, it had meant giving up every shred of control, becoming accountable to him for every minute of her time. She had no intentions of putting herself in such a position again.

By the time she rejoined James, document case under her arm, her smile was coolly professional. "Shall we go? My car's parked outside."

"We'll be more comfortable in mine." He indicated a sleek black Branxton Turbo that managed to make her sedan, of which she was normally quite proud, look positively shabby. How did you make a car gleam like this anyway?

"But I know the way," she countered, wondering why it was suddenly important to her to win this round. She told herself she was being practical, insisting on her own transportation, but the reason went deeper. For some reason,

James Langford set her senses on automatic alert, although she couldn't think why.

It wasn't his stature or his wealth. In the property management business she'd learned to operate at all levels. And oddly enough, she felt her honor was safe with him, although he'd probably find such an old-fashioned notion laughable, if not a slight to his manhood.

No, there was something else about him which counseled caution, even if it was only her imagination, which seemed to be working overtime today.

She was mildly surprised when he slid into the passenger seat of her car without further discussion, reaching across to open her door from the inside. He seemed to take up a great deal of space inside the compact car, she noticed.

"Have you inspected many properties in Sydney?" she asked, trying to switch into professional mode before her thoughts ran away with her again. Around James it seemed all too easy.

"My deputy has looked at a number of them, but none entirely suits the company's needs."

She cast a sidelong look at him, almost disappointed that the conversation had switched to business so readily. "What are your company's needs exactly?"

"A top location, naturally. A substantial parcel of land. And a property that has heritage value so our visiting executives gain some sense of the Australian character while they're here."

"Then you're not buying for yourself?"

He shook his head. "Not to live in, no. I already keep a penthouse in the city and my main residence on the border of the Watagan State Forest, a few miles north of Sydney."

Her eyes widened with delighted surprise. "I know it. My grandparents lived not far from Wollombi. I used to hand-feed kangaroos outside their back door."

His interest was clearly piqued. "Perhaps I know them."

A pang shot through her. "They died some years ago, within months of each other. I haven't been up that way in a long time."

She couldn't have been more than fourteen the last time she stayed with her grandparents, although she'd visited them often as an adult. The memory of walking through lush green rain forests and trying to carry on a conversation over the summer evening anthem of cicadas remained with her.

Was it because her grandparents' house was the only real home she'd known as a child? Her parents had been botanists, well enough known in their respective fields, but genteelly impoverished. Most of their time had been spent out in the field while their only daughter was farmed out to relatives, since they couldn't afford boarding-school fees.

After her father succumbed to a rare tropical disease on an expedition to South America, her mother had retired to the south coast of New South Wales, amid a jungle of a garden where she grew medicinal herbs.

By then mother and daughter were so estranged that Zoe couldn't imagine living with her mother. Fortunately by then she was working as a nanny, living with her charge's family, so the question never arose. Her mother wouldn't have enjoyed an enforced family existence any more than Zoe herself would.

"And your husband?"

James's voice snapped Zoe back to the present with a jolt, banishing the floodgate of memories opened by his mention of her childhood home. "My husband died two years ago in a car accident," she said quietly.

She accepted James's murmured condolences with a nod, not feeling inclined to explain to him that the only sorrow she felt on Andrew's behalf was over his untimely death, not to any sense of loss of her own.

It had taken her months to stop feeling guilty because

Andrew's death had freed her from his obsessive jealousy. At first she had wondered what sort of woman she was, not to grieve for her husband, until Julie had reminded her sternly that Andrew himself had killed her love for him.

"I noticed the toys on your front lawn," James went on. "How many children do you have?"

Surprise shot through her. Usually male clients weren't the slightest bit interested in her domestic affairs once they established whether or not she was married. She told herself James was only making polite conversation.

She paid attention to the road. The turnoff to the Strathfield place wasn't far. Then she became aware that James was regarding her steadily, awaiting her answer.

"I don't have any children of my own," she said flatly, wondering at the same time why she was telling him more than he probably wanted to know. "I have a foster daughter, Genie, who's at playgroup this afternoon."

He moved restively, his athletic body tensing against the restraining seat belt. Already regretting his interest in her family, she concluded. Well, he needn't worry. She wasn't about to drag out a sheaf of baby pictures.

His next comment caught her off guard. "I had a little girl of my own. They can be a source of great joy."

His use of the past tense didn't escape her. Had his child died? Her own all-consuming love for Genie made it easy to understand the anguish the loss of a child would mean. "Did something happen to her?" she asked gently.

Her sidelong glance caught the hardening of his jaw. "Yes, but it wasn't some childhood ailment. That would have made some sense."

Her knuckles whitened around the steering wheel. Oh, no, not a kidnapping. His prominence in the business world made the possibility frighteningly real. "Then what?"

"My wife decided our marriage wasn't to her liking,"

he said. "She took my daughter to another country and used an assumed name to make sure I couldn't find them."

The pain in his voice vibrated through Zoe. Although she and Andrew had never had a child, she could imagine her despair if he had done such an awful thing to her. She blinked hard. "Do you know where they are?"

Her peripheral vision caught his taut nod. "It's taken me a long time, but I do now."

He added no more details, leaving her to speculate that wherever his wife had gone, there was no chance he could retrieve his daughter. Otherwise, she suspected, he would move heaven and earth to do so.

"How old is your foster daughter?" he asked.

The strain in his voice tugged at her. Far from being a polite question, it suggested that he wanted to discuss her child, perhaps to distract himself from thinking of his own loss.

"She's four and a half," she said, obliging him. "She starts school in a few months. I don't know how I'll get through the days without her."

"You and your husband never had children of your own?"

"It...didn't work out for us. We had a few problems," she added with difficulty. Even now it was hard to talk about her marriage, which had started so well until Andrew's true character emerged. "Genie has more than made up. She's an adorable child, full of mischief like most children her age, but so loving that I can't stay annoyed with her for long."

James folded his arms across his broad chest. "Does that mean you spoil her?"

She flashed him a wry smile before returning her attention to the road. "Is it possible to spoil a four-year-old? She doesn't get everything her own way, but when it comes to loving her, I don't believe you can go overboard, do you?''

His weight shifted on the seat bedside her, attracting her attention. In profile, his features were half in shadow. "Unfortunately I didn't get the chance to find out."

Horrified with herself, she fell silent. What was she thinking of, going on and on about the joys of parenthood when it only reminded him of his loss? He had started the conversation, she told herself, but she could have framed her answers with a little more sensitivity. With relief she sighted their turnoff. "We're almost there."

If he sensed her relief, he gave no indication. Nor did he take more than a cursory interest in his first sight of the mansion as the electronically operated gates swung open to admit them. Was he acting disinterested as a prelude to some hard bargaining? He had seemed far more animated when discussing their children than he did as they got out of the car and approached the house, their footsteps crunching on the freshly raked gravel driveway.

Apart from a caretaker who lived in a cottage on the grounds, the property was unoccupied. Her sense of unease returned. She put it down to the silence settling around them as soon as she switched off the engine. "Would you like to see the house or the grounds first?" she asked, unaccountably hoping he would choose to explore the garden.

"The house," he decided. "There are six bedroom suites, I understand."

Her unsettled feeling was probably due to the discussion about his missing daughter, she thought. Knowing how she would feel under the same circumstances was bound to affect her. She was thankful to be able to switch the conversation to the virtues of the mansion.

He responded in kind, asking shrewd questions about the house, its history and the land surrounding it. By the time she had shown him everything, over an hour had gone by.

Apart from his questions, his demeanor gave her no clues as to whether or not she had a sale.

Somehow she also found herself talking more about her own life, she noticed. His questioning was so subtle that it wasn't until the inspection was almost over that she realized they'd talked more about her than about the house.

"If you want to see the house again, I'll be happy to arrange a second inspection," she told him as they walked back to her car.

"There's no need. I'll take it."

She could hardly believe her ears. A million-dollar property and he would take it, just like that? The commission from this one sale alone would take care of most of Genie's needs for some time to come.

"You will?" she said, professionalism failing slightly as elation gripped her. "That's great. I had a feeling it was right for you when you explained your company's requirements."

He nodded briskly. "The company will want to make some changes. Add a few more modern conveniences and more secure car parking, of course."

"I'm authorized to discuss offers," she assured him, mentally calculating the cost of the improvements he'd outlined. No doubt he would expect the final selling price to reflect them.

He named a figure only slightly below the asking price, which she had privately decided was above market value anyway. Evidently James agreed with her because his offer was exactly the one she would have made in his shoes. She was sure her clients would accept his offer without further negotiation.

At her car she swung around to face him. "I'll call the vendors on the way back to my place. I'm sure your offer will be acceptable, so we can go to my office and get the preliminary paperwork under way this afternoon if you like.''

He braced an arm against the roof of her car, meeting her gaze with disturbing directness. A woman could drown in those blue pools, she thought. She had the uncanny sensation that he knew everything there was to know about her—every secret, every dark place. And found it intriguing.

She shook her head slightly to clear it. More fantasies, Zoe? What was the matter with her today? It must be the thrill of making such an important sale. She refused to believe her state of mind could be blamed on James's effect on her.

His slightly lopsided smile warmed her. ''Do you have the offer document with you?''

She nodded and drew it out of her portfolio. He barely glanced at the fine print before writing in the price they'd discussed and scrawling his signature at the bottom. It was as firm and bold as everything else about him, she noticed.

''There, you have my offer in writing,'' he confirmed. ''Everything else will be handled by my deputy, Brian Dengate, at my head office.''

A faint sense of disappointment rippled through her. So he wasn't to be involved in the purchase beyond today's inspection. She dismissed the thought with surprising difficulty. ''In that case, it's been a pleasure doing business with you, James.'' She slid into the driver's seat and he got in beside her. ''I'll have you back at your car in fifteen minutes.''

''There's no hurry,'' he said, catching her unawares. ''I still have some matters to discuss with you.''

Unaccountably her spirits lifted. He probably wanted to question her about the local zoning laws and heritage listing requirements, but it didn't seem to matter. She only knew she was happy to continue the conversation.

They had reached her house before she realized he hadn't asked any of his questions, talking instead about inconsequential matters. "Would you like to come in for coffee?" she offered and found herself holding her breath as she waited for his answer.

He nodded, his face impassive. She couldn't tell whether he was as drawn to her as she was to him, but at least he hadn't refused. Her step was light as she led the way inside.

Her home was modest but well-cared-for. Not what he would be accustomed to, she thought as they stepped over toys in the hallway to reach the living room. She'd decorated it herself with cream wallpaper, a handwoven Mexican rug and a few inventive touches such as a pottery jar holding giant paper sunflowers.

James settled himself on the sofa while she fetched coffee and homemade walnut cake. But he refused the cake and his coffee sat untouched at his elbow as he leaned toward her. "I have something to tell you, Zoe."

He looked so serious that alarm shrilled through her. "If you're worried about the heritage listing—"

"This isn't about the property." He forestalled her. "It's about Genevieve."

For a moment the name confused her, then the truth dawned. "You mean Genie. What about her?"

James reached into his jacket pocket and withdrew a sheaf of documents. "There's no easy way to tell you this, but there's absolutely no doubt. The child you know as Genie is my daughter, Genevieve. All the proof you need is in these reports."

Chapter Two

Zoe felt as if she had stepped off a sandbank into deep water, which was rapidly closing over her head. Her skin turned icy and every breath became a huge effort. This was how it felt to drown, she thought, as if seeing her own reaction from a distance.

"She's *what?*"

"She's the daughter who was taken from me eighteen months ago. Her real name is Genevieve Matilda Langford."

The drowning sensation went on and on, but there was also the sense of seeing herself from above as Zoe dispassionately noted every detail of her pose which miraculously hadn't altered.

She sat frozen with one slim leg crossed over the other in a calm precision which now seemed to mock her other self, watching from above. She had actually thought that James wanted to prolong their meeting for other than business reasons. The truth chilled her beyond belief. All his interest in her marriage and her child had been designed to draw her out, to confirm what he must already have known. Like a panther toying with its prey, he had been waiting for the right moment to deliver his devastating news.

With an agonizing rush she inhabited her body again, feeling every nuance of the pain squeezing her heart relentlessly. Her bones felt liquid and she knew she couldn't have stood up to save her life.

She was aware of James's tension as if they were connected by invisible wires. The denials she held back in her throat vibrated along the connection like the ghostly echo of a million callers down a telephone line. He watched her silently, apparently waiting for her to say something. But her mind was gripped by so much pain and confusion that speech seemed beyond her.

He had come to claim Genie. The realization burned through her tortured mind, erasing all other coherent thoughts. Her beautiful, beloved daughter belonged to him.

It couldn't be true. It was all some terrible nightmare from which she would awaken at any moment. She would feel Genie's insistent tug on her hair and she would pry her eyes open to protest that it was too early to get up. "But the sun's awake, Mummy," Genie would insist. Laughing, Zoe would swing her legs over the edge of the bed and catch the child's squirming body to her for a good-morning hug.

"Zoe? Are you all right?"

It wasn't Genie's voice but James's vibrant baritone, which banished the vision and replaced it with a harsh reality that refused to be denied. Without knowing it, Zoe had squeezed her eyes shut. She opened them now, knowing that the full extent of her pain would be visible to James who was reaching out to her.

She shrugged away his offered hand. "I'm all right. I just...this is...I don't know what to say."

He looked down at his long-fingered hands then back to

her again, his cerulean gaze mirroring her torment. "There's nothing to say. You've done a wonderful job of taking care of her."

She recoiled from the decisive edge in his voice. Done, past tense. She found her voice with an effort. "You make it sound as if it's over."

His head jerked up. "You know it is, Zoe. You were only able to foster her while her family couldn't be traced. Now she has family. I'm her father and she belongs with me."

"But Ruth told me..." Zoe clamped her jaw shut on the accusations welling up inside her. Ruth had managed to convince her that Genie's father was an unfeeling brute who didn't care about his wife and daughter.

James gave a resigned sigh. "Whatever she told you about me is probably as much a fabrication as the identity she used."

Confusion coiled through Zoe. Throughout the house inspection she'd begun to feel compassion toward him. Yet Ruth had described him as hard and uncaring, too preoccupied with business affairs to have much time for his family. Which was the real James Langford? she wondered.

His public image was of a stop-at-nothing entrepreneur who had built a global communications business from nothing. The Aussie Bulldozer, *Time* magazine had called him. Now Zoe was standing in the bulldozer's path, and he would go over her if she forced him to. But he would not be stopped, that much she knew with a numbing certainty.

She clutched at another straw. "You said your wife took your daughter to another country." Perhaps this was some ghastly case of mistaken identity.

He nodded. "She did—Australia. My company was setting up a satellite communications network in the Middle East when we met. Ruth was handling security for the project. Neither of us planned on what happened, but it was a forbidding, lonely place for a foreigner. The political situation was delicate, and we couldn't move outside our headquarters without an armed escort." He gave a wry grimace. "In a situation like that, people turn to each other and form bonds more quickly than they might under normal conditions."

Her throat felt gravelly. "You were married in the Middle East?"

"We hadn't planned to until Ruth became pregnant." He frowned at Zoe's sharply indrawn breath. "Don't look so scandalized. We took precautions, but Ruth suffered a bout of food poisoning and her contraception failed. Ruth wasn't really the marrying kind, and I doubt if she would have said yes if not for her pregnancy."

From her short acquaintance with his wife, Zoe suspected he was right. Ruth had given the impression that she enjoyed flaunting her power over men, but hated being pinned down for long. As a mother, she took little interest in the childish milestones Zoe had dutifully reported to her each day.

In many ways Ruth had reminded Zoe of a butterfly, moving restlessly from flower to flower, hating to be impeded in her travels. She hadn't struck Zoe as a woman for whom marriage and motherhood were natural choices.

James watched the expressions moving over her face. "I see you know what she was like."

"I only knew her for a short time when she moved into an apartment across the road," Zoe explained, her voice deepened by the ache in her throat. "She called herself Ruth Sullivan and said she was working as a courier in the city. Sometimes she left Genie with me overnight, so I was accustomed to having her sleep here. But when Ruth didn't return to collect her for two days, I went to her address to see if she was ill. There was no answer and her neighbors hadn't seen her in days, so I contacted the police."

"Who traced her movements and discovered she'd been killed in that sailing accident," James supplied. His tone said he was still adjusting to the discovery. In the midst of her own desolation, Zoe felt an unexpected wave of compassion for him.

"According to the police, she was involved with a pretty reckless crowd who encouraged her to try all sorts of dangerous sports," Zoe added.

His sigh of resignation hissed between them. "Knowing Ruth, she wouldn't have needed much encouragement. She enjoyed living on the edge. It made her feel alive. Working in the Middle East suited her need for adventure. I should have known better than to expect her to settle into domesticity with me."

"What happened between you?" Through her hurt, Zoe felt compelled to ask the question, to know everything about Genie's brief life before she came to Zoe. Until now she'd only had Ruth's account to go by.

A shadow crossed his chiseled features. "When we found out she was pregnant, I suggested returning to Australia so the baby could be born here." He lapsed into a long, nerve-stretching silence before continuing. "For a while, things seemed to work out, but Ruth became restless. I had to return to the Middle East to complete our contract. Ruth wanted to come with me, but Genevieve was not yet two. I tried to cut my trip as short as I could. I was only supposed to be gone for a month."

His deep voice cracked. The pain caused by his memories enfolded Zoe as if it was her own—which in a way, it was. But for these events triggered half a world away, she would not now be facing the worst moment of her life.

"She couldn't wait a month?" she managed to ask, saying the unsayable for him. How could any woman, the mother of his child, not wait a lifetime for the man she loved, if that was what was required?

"In the end...circumstances...intervened. It was much longer than a month before I was able to return," he rasped. "By the time I got back she was gone, taking my daughter with her."

A distant part of her mind noticed that he made no attempt to explain what circumstances had kept him away. Was it the pressure of business? Or, heaven forbid, another woman? Neither were excusable when he had a wife and baby waiting for him at home.

Whatever had happened was none of her business except as it concerned Genie, she told herself. He was probably only telling her the story at all to help her understand how Genie came to be in Zoe's care. The crazy part was she *did* understand. In his shoes she would have done everything in her power to find her child, just as James had. But the mother in her railed against it with every breath in her body. How in the name of all that was right and true could she face giving Genie up?

"I know this must be hard for you," James conceded. Distantly she registered that he felt badly about what he was doing. Yet she also sensed that nothing she said or did, no amount of tears or pleading, would change his course any more than one rock can alter the eventual course of a mighty river.

"Hard?" she echoed, her eyes blurring as she lifted them to him. "This goes way beyond hard, all the way to impossible. I doubt if you have the slightest idea how hard this is, Mr. Langford."

It registered that familiarity had gone, along with any sense of the attraction she had begun to feel toward him.

He gestured toward the documents lying between them on the coffee table. "Are you sure I don't know how this feels? If you come back to my office, I can show you files stacked higher than that table with reports and false leads, rumors and red herrings, as well as hard intelligence gathered inch by painstaking inch since the day Genevieve was taken away from me.'' His jaw hardened. ''So don't tell me I can't understand how it feels.''

The difference was that he had had longer to adjust to the situation, if that helped any. Somehow she doubted it. And if he got his way, she would have to live without Genie a lot longer than James had. She forced herself to ask, ''What do you intend to do now?''

He paced to the window, parting the curtain to survey the suburban vista beyond before swinging back to face her. Compassion softened the lines etched around his features, but his eyes shone with purpose. ''I intend to get to know my child, be a father to her again. We've been kept apart quite long enough.''

Her mind refused to deal with any of this. Even acknowledging that she had heard him would lead to discussing ways and means. Suddenly she understood how bereaved people could prattle on about trivial matters, anything to avoid facing the reality of their loss.

She locked her hands around her knees, her thoughts stupidly sticking on the Strathfield mansion. Why had he wanted to see it if he had no real interest in the property? ''This whole meeting was a sham, wasn't it?'' she said woodenly. ''Have you enjoyed playing cat and mouse with me all afternoon, relishing the moment when you could spring your trap?''

Anger flashed in his vivid gaze. ''It wasn't a sham,'' he denied. ''My company does intend to purchase a property where we can accommodate visiting executives. But you're right, it wasn't why I made the appointment with you.'' He glanced around. ''I wanted to see for myself what you were like and how my child has been living.''

Zoe drew herself up to her full height, anger running like a river through her. She had a fair idea how inadequate her modest home must seem to someone with his background.

"How dare you come here and check me out in such an underhanded way?" she demanded. "I may not have your resources, but Genie has wanted for nothing while she's been in my care."

James's face clouded. He remained as still as a statue at the window, but his hands balled into fists at his sides. "If our roles were reversed, you'd have done exactly the same thing. Fortunately the team of private investigators I've had on the case since she disappeared assure me that Genevieve has flourished in your care. What I've seen for myself this afternoon bears it out, so you have no need to be angry on that score. On the contrary, I'm eternally grateful for all you've done."

His appreciation fell on deaf ears as she recoiled almost physically at the idea of being investigated. It reminded her all too vividly of Andrew's endless suspicions and questioning, even to the extent of watching her from his car to make sure she was indeed going to the supermarket and not to a meeting with another man.

"You've had me under investigation?" she repeated, revulsion sending shivers arrowing down her spine. "It didn't occur to you to simply knock on the door and ask me anything you wanted to know?"

He spread his fingers wide. "I didn't wish to confront you until I was sure of my facts. Over the months I've had to deal with a string of false leads and disappointments. If the child had turned out not to be my daughter, you would never have known of my interest."

Iced water slid along her veins. "I can't believe you had me watched and every detail of my life investigated without me knowing anything about it. It's almost..." She sprang to her feet, her mind groping for the right word. "Voyeuristic. How many other people have you spied on without their knowledge, pawing through the details of their lives?"

He was beside her in two long strides, his hands firm as

they gripped her upper arms and he forced her to look at him. "Stop this, Zoe. I know you're shocked and you have every right to be. But I refuse to apologize for using every trick in the book, dirty or otherwise, to find my child. She is what matters here, not my feelings and not yours."

To her horror she felt two tears slide gracelessly down her hot cheeks. He swore beneath his breath and his hold tightened until she was cradled against the hard wall of his chest. His fingers wound through her hair in a comforting caress. "Don't, please."

It was the sort of embrace she might have used to comfort Genie. Yet without Zoe being sure when or how it happened, it swiftly turned into something more. She knew she was vulnerable and her judgment was not to be trusted at this moment, but neither could she deny the lightning flash of awareness that arced between them as his hands slid down her neck and settled on her trembling shoulders.

It came as absolutely no surprise when his lips found the top of her head. Rather, it felt almost inevitable, as if the awareness she had sensed the moment she opened the door to him was no more than a prelude to finding herself in his arms.

Her pulses went haywire as his lips traveled to her forehead. Slowly the shudder of suppressed sobs became something deeper, more elemental. It took every bit of self-control she possessed to remember who he was and why she was in his embrace.

Genie.

Desperately she focused on her child's name and felt her strength of will flowing back. As soon as she placed her palms against the padded muscle of his shoulders, he released her. But he remained no more than a step away as if expecting her to crumble again, his hair-trigger reflexes set to catch her.

"I'm sorry," she said as if apologizing only for the momentary weakness.

His quick, wry smile stressed his understanding of her need to deny what they both knew had just happened. It was an explosive situation. Emotions were running at feverpitch. His expression told her he didn't believe she was apologizing for her weakness any more than she did, but he was decent enough to let it serve. "No need for apologies," he said, finally moving away so she could release the breath she'd been unaware of holding. "It's a tough situation all around."

Holding all the cards, he could afford to be generous. Still she couldn't dismiss the gentleness with which he'd held her or the fiery way his lips had burned through her skin when he kissed her.

Spying on her to gain his own ends made him no better than Andrew, she reminded herself although it was an effort. The thought gave her the courage to meet his gaze. "Will you give me some time? I need to examine your documents..." Her voice trailed off. The paperwork was almost certainly in order. A man like James Langford wouldn't make his move until he knew it was the right one. She was the one who needed time to come to terms with a life forever changed.

Then she needed to prepare Genie to deal with another huge upheaval in a short life that had already seen more disruption than was good for her. That was going to be the most heart-tearing job of all.

James nodded reluctantly. "Take whatever time you need. The papers are self-explanatory, but you can ask me anything and I'll do my best to answer."

Only one question burned in her mind: how could he do this to her? It was the one question she couldn't ask and he wouldn't answer. Because he had already dismissed it as irrelevant. She was a painful but necessary step in his quest to retrieve his child.

"In the meantime," he continued implacably, "I want to see Genevieve."

Zoe felt the color drain from her face. "You aren't going to simply tell her who you are?"

James locked gazes with her. "What do you think I am? No, don't answer. If it helps you to cast me as the villain, go right ahead. But it won't dissuade me from getting to know her again so she can accept me into her life. There will be time enough for the whole story when she's ready to cope with it."

He was being fairer than she had any right to expect. And he was right, she *was* trying to cast him as the villain, if only to have a target for her distress. The real villain was Ruth for involving them all in this terrible situation in which there could be no real winners.

Zoe nodded painfully. "You have the right to see her, of course." More than she herself did if it came down to it. Inspiration came to her. "I'm taking her to our local street fair on Saturday. One of the highlights is a charity auction I'm involved in. Could you meet us there? It won't seem as strange to her as if you came here."

His expression underwent a sea change. Too late she realized how revealing her suggestion must look to him. She had as good as admitted that she wasn't in the habit of introducing strange men to Genie. Her pride balked at such an admission. Would he think she had succumbed to his embrace because she was starved for affection? It shouldn't matter what he thought. She only knew it did.

"I mean, I don't want to give her the wrong idea about you and me…about us." She stumbled on.

A glimmer of amusement lit his vivid blue gaze. "Heaven forbid she should get the wrong idea about…us," he said with a mocking lilt. Then he drew himself back to business. "The street fair is a good idea. I would wish to see her sooner, but perhaps we all need the time to adjust."

For a moment his face became shadowed and a depth of longing almost beyond bearing darkened his eyes. The ache around Zoe's heart grew as she realized she was asking him to wait yet another couple of days for a reunion that had already been postponed beyond most people's endurance.

It was on the tip of her tongue to say, "Wait, she'll be home in a little while. You don't have to endure another day without seeing her." But it was her own yearning speaking, so she closed her lips on the betraying words. No doubt he would have accepted her offer with alacrity, and part of her admitted the justice in making it. But she wasn't ready yet. According him his due as Genie's father was harder than anything she'd ever been asked to do.

It spelled the end of her life with her child. The end of her world.

The offer remained unspoken as she walked him to the door. She was distantly aware that they made some sort of arrangement to meet at the fair, but the details barely registered with her. Somehow she knew that James wouldn't forget. He didn't have her reasons.

The documents proving Genie's parentage stared up at her in mute accusation when she went back inside. She looked at them for a long time before forcing herself to reach for the folder.

Chapter Three

To Zoe it felt like a century since James had dropped his bombshell about Genie, but in reality only two days had passed by the time the day of the street fair dawned. They were the longest two days of Zoe's life. Over and over she asked herself why she had agreed to meet James at the fair?

She had little choice, she acknowledged as she went through the motions of getting ready to go. The alternative—inviting James to her home again—was even more unsettling.

He had a right to see his child. Even Zoe couldn't deny the fact. But he didn't have to see her under Zoe's roof. A public place was better, she told herself. Neutral ground. He would see what a wonderful mother she was and decide to leave Genie where she was.

And pigs might fly.

She started as a small figure appeared at her bedroom door. "I'm ready, Mummy. Can we go now?" The child jiggled up and down with impatience.

Zoe swallowed the maternal pride that threatened to

swamp her. "As soon as I'm ready, sweetheart. I won't be long."

Genie's features creased with suspicion. "You're wearing your best dress, and your hair's all funny and crinkly. You won't be able to go on the Ferris wheel with me."

Zoe dropped to her knees beside the little girl. "Of course I will. I felt like dressing up and curling my hair because...well, just because." Impressing James Langford had absolutely nothing to do with it, she told herself.

Genie's nose twitched. "You smell different, too."

Okay, so she had used some of the Chanel No. 5 one of her clients had given her last Christmas. "Must you be so observant?" she asked Genie, hugging her tightly.

Genie struggled free. "What does surfant mean?"

Zoe stood up, smoothing down her one and only designer dress, a simple sheath in a pale avocado silk. The severely tailored lines were softened by a row of amber beading stitched into the neckline. Her neighbor Julie called it a drop-dead dress. "In it, you can tell anyone to drop dead," she'd explained when Zoe hesitated over spending the money. Was that the reason Zoe wanted to wear it today, to put her on a more equal footing with James? She wouldn't consider that it had anything to do with his attractiveness as a man.

"Observant means you notice everything," she explained wryly as she finished dusting fine powder over her even features. All right, so she was overdressed for a street fair, but today she needed all the morale boosting she could get.

Coral lipstick outlined a smile even she had to admit looked shaky. She forced her lips into a more convincing arc and swung around. "Let's go."

There was no sign of James when they reached the main street, which had been closed off for the day. A crowd already thronged the fairground attractions and street stalls, but she could have spotted James in any crowd. Not only did his unusual height make him stand out, but he radiated an aura of power and authority that drew all eyes like a magnet.

Zoe's nerves were now strung wire-taut. She was glad when Genie begged for a turn on a huge inflatable jumping castle that already held several shrieking children.

"I'll sit over there and have a cup of coffee where I can watch you," she told the excited child as she paid for a ticket. She chose a seat at an outdoor table surrounded by lush green potted plants and sank gratefully onto a wooden chair. "Cappuccino, thank you," she told the waiter who appeared at her side.

"Make it two," a deep voice contributed.

Reaction blistered through her as James took a seat opposite her. She had almost convinced herself he wasn't coming, that everything would be all right. Now he was here and her stomach churned. She regretted not forcing herself to have some breakfast this morning. His presence made her feel abruptly light-headed.

"You look pale. Perhaps you should eat something," he suggested with uncanny insight.

"I'm fine," she denied. Anything she tried to eat under these conditions would probably refuse to stay down.

He nodded distractedly, his gaze sweeping the attractions around them. "Where is Genevieve?"

Her flashing glance gave him the answer. His eyes followed her gaze to the inflatable castle where Genie bounced up and down, tumbling over then righting herself, all the while shrieking with delight.

His reaction was a sharply indrawn breath. "The photographs didn't begin to show how beautiful she is."

Against her will, Zoe's gaze lifted to his taut features. They radiated a look she'd seen in the mirror countless times—a look of pure parental pride. Pain pierced her like an arrow. She hadn't wanted to see such a look on his face. It would be easier to bear if Ruth had been right and he didn't care.

But it was all too apparent that he did and his intent expression revealed just how much. "She is beautiful in nature as well as in looks," she agreed softly, unable to keep her anguish from seeping into her tone.

He brought his gaze back to Zoe with obvious reluctance, as if it was all he could do to tear his eyes away from the happy child. "You've done a fine job raising her," he said, his tone husky with emotion.

Zoe had promised herself she wouldn't beg, but the words came out anyway. "Then why not let me go on doing it?"

A waiter placed coffee in front of them, obscuring James's face for a moment, but there was no mistaking the challenge in his voice. "If our roles were reversed, could you walk away?"

She sprinkled sugar over the cocoa frosting of the cappuccino and watched the froth start to dissipate like so many of her hopes and dreams. "No, I couldn't."

A muscle worked along his jawline. "Yet you expect me to be able to?"

"You've been out of her life for almost two years, two years in which I've been the only mother she's known. You said yourself I've done a good job." She didn't add that they were years in which she had fixed him in her mind as an uncaring monster. Confusion spilled through her as she was forced to confront the reality of a man determined to get his child back at all costs. Hardly the image of a monster.

"It doesn't change the facts. I'm her father," he said, confirming her turbulent thoughts. He cupped both hands around his coffee, then flexed his fingers as if reaching a decision. "I hoped we could reach an agreement without this, Zoe, but your stubbornness leaves me no option."

Iced water trickled down her spine. "To do what?"

He looked up, his eyes alight with purpose. "I've been checking. I thought you simply sold real estate, but you hold a much more senior job in property management, don't you?"

What was he getting at? "Yes," she admitted cautiously. "I'm only handling the sale of the Strathfield place as a favor to the owner."

"For whom you manage several apartment blocks?" She nodded again. "Which means you collect the rents, find tenants, solve their problems and generally take care of things for the owner. It must take up a lot of your time."

"I have plenty of time to be a mother to Genie, if that's what you're implying."

His eyes snapped fire. "I'm not implying anything. I'm stating facts. Your work takes up a good deal of time."

A hollow sensation invaded her. His spies must have been thorough for him to know so much about her. "It doesn't mean Genie's neglected," she asserted. "I love her. I work hard to give her everything she deserves. As a foster mother, I get a welfare payment but it doesn't stretch to the life I want for her."

Over the rim of the coffee cup, his expression remained unforgiving. "I would never suggest you neglect her. Being unavailable might be a better way to put it."

His comment plunged to the heart of her deepest fears. Was it better to earn a good living and give Genie the start in life she deserved, or deprive her materially in order to be there as a mother to her? For Ruth there had been no such dilemma. Her own needs had always come first. Perhaps James was thinking of Ruth when he leveled his accusation at Zoe. If so, how could she convince him that she was different from Ruth? Anger overcame her despair. "I can't believe you'd use such a weapon against me."

"I'll use whatever it takes to get my daughter back."

He meant it, Zoe saw from the fire in his eyes and the unyielding set of his jaw.

For one insane moment she wondered what it would be like to have him on her side, instead of as the enemy. Nothing would be allowed to prevail against him. The thought seized her with such a powerful sense of longing that she was shaken. During her marriage to Andrew she had never felt he was truly her ally. With James there would be no doubt. But in this instance they were never going to be on the same side so she was wishing for the moon.

"Mummy, did you see me jumping?" Zoe's heart turned over as Genie skittered to a halt beside her chair, her eyes widening as she noticed the man sharing the table.

Zoe slipped an arm around the child's waist and drew her closer. "You were very good, sweetheart. Now say hello to..." Mr. Langford? Your father? Her mind blanked on the possibilities.

He smiled and offered the child his hand. There was a faint tremor in his voice as he said, "I'm James, and I'm *very* glad to see you, Genevieve."

For one heart-stopping moment Zoe thought Genie was going to recognize James. So did he, she saw from the tension that flared in his expression. But the moment passed with no further reaction from Genie. The child turned back to Zoe. "We're still going on the Ferris wheel, aren't we?"

"We'll go together," James decided, standing up. He brushed the child's dark hair with his fingers and Zoe caught her breath when she glimpsed the look of wonder in his eyes. She thought she saw him swallow hard before the shutters came down again on his expression.

The child led the way to the line for the fair's main attraction. As Zoe hurried to keep up, she said softly, "I'm sorry she showed no signs of recognizing you. You were hoping she would, weren't you?''

His closed expression betrayed nothing, but she hadn't forgotten his transparent look of a moment ago. It was getting harder and harder to connect him with the portrait Ruth had painted of him. Which was the real James Langford? she asked herself again. "I'm prepared to give it time," he conceded.

In spite of her inner turmoil, Zoe couldn't suppress a surge of compassion for him. Used to having the business world at his command, he couldn't command the outcome this time. His face in that unguarded moment, and her own experience of motherhood told her how much he must want to.

"Eighteen months is a long time when you're not yet five," she murmured.

He paused in front of the ticket booth and gave her a wry look. "It's a long time at any age."

The three of them were seated in one of the small, gently swaying compartments of the Ferris wheel by the time Zoe got her confused feelings under control, on the surface at least. Given his avowed intention to take Genie from her, how could she feel anything but hostility toward him?

Yet seated across from the two of them, watching the wind whip the dark strands of hair across his forehead, she felt an unwilling empathy with him. After her experience with Andrew, the last thing she wanted was to feel this way toward any man. Next she'd be admitting to herself how attractive James was, when she should know by now that attractiveness didn't always go hand in hand with a pleasant demeanor. Andrew had been attractive enough and charming as long as he was the one in control.

But James wasn't like Andrew, she'd stake almost anything on it. His gentleness toward Genie spoke volumes. Even his readiness to delay his reunion with her to give

Zoe time to adjust was in his favor. Could she have sacrificed as much?

Determinedly she slammed a door in her mind on the list of his virtues. They wouldn't stop him from taking Genie away. The thought brought a sob to Zoe's throat, which she held back by sheer force of will.

Fully laden at last, the wheel began to turn steadily, carrying them high above the streetscape. Genie's face reflected her fascination at the bird's-eye view she was getting of her world. Zoe's stomach clenched at the sight of Genie's tiny hand creeping into James's. The child was unaware of taking his hand. She had done it automatically.

Did some part of Genie remember her connection with the big man at her side? She was usually shy with strangers, but with James she seemed to have few reservations. At the sight of the two of them together, Zoe felt the color slide from her cheeks. Was she glimpsing the future?

James noticed her sudden pallor. "Do heights bother you?"

Unable to restrain herself, she glanced at their linked hands. "The height isn't my problem."

A shadow crossed his features. "Somehow I thought not."

Thankfully the ride wasn't as interminable as it felt and they were soon back on the ground, making another circuit of the stalls at Genie's insistence. "James hasn't seen them *all* yet," she defended when Zoe mentioned that James might not share Genie's fascination with the fairground attractions.

"But I do. I'm enjoying every minute of this," he insisted.

He certainly looked as if he was, or else he was a superb actor, Zoe thought. Watching him pay close attention to Genie's explanation of how the shooting gallery worked, Zoe resisted the urge to be impressed. He might look like one of the dozens of fathers around them, out to give their children a good time, but nothing was further from the truth as far as she was concerned.

Nevertheless she found it hard not to warm to his enthusiasm as he paid for a rifle and round of blank ammunition to try his luck at the shooting gallery. He had handled a real rifle, she concluded, watching the efficient way he held and sighted the toy weapon. His tanned forearm cradled the gun with casual expertise. His left hand curled around the barrel while his right stroked the trigger. Resting the stock against his cheek he squeezed off the first shots.

As the gun went off, something else exploded inside Zoe at the same moment. Each report vibrated through her as if aimed directly at her. The final one impacted around her heart and she drew a strangled breath. What was going on here?

"James, you did it, you won!"

Genie's cry of joy brought Zoe back to reality. She forced a smile as the vendor handed Genie a furry pink dog, which she hugged tightly, her eyes shining. At the sight of the big man and the tiny child half-hidden behind the toy dog, Zoe's heart turned over. Every move he made seemed destined to threaten her immunity to him. It was all she could do to sound matter-of-fact as she said, "What do you say to James?"

"Thank you," came the response muffled by toy-dog fur.

"Thank *you* for showing me what to do," he said, earning another adoring look from the child. His smile could have lit up the street fair all by itself. Despite her resolution not to respond, Zoe found his high spirits disturbingly infectious. And all because he had pleased a little girl.

Ruth must have been out of her mind, Zoe thought, then just as quickly checked the thought. Charming he might be, but he was also a man with an agenda in which Zoe was the main casualty.

"What's next?" he asked, his sweeping gaze encompassing the busy street.

"The action," Genie declared. "Mummy's going to be in it."

One dark eyebrow slanted upward and he fixed her with an amused look. "The action?"

Zoe felt her color heighten. "She means the auction. Local businesses have donated goods and services to be auctioned to raise funds for new playground equipment for the park. You wouldn't find it very interesting."

His curiosity was obviously piqued. "If you're going to be in it, I wouldn't miss it for the world. Right, Genevieve?"

The child giggled. "Why do you keep calling me Genevieve when my name's Genie?"

Instantly James's face clouded and Zoe felt a pang of sympathy for him as she read the distress in his gaze. They'd all been having such a good time, and James had clearly been so taken with Genie that he'd allowed himself to forget how far he still had to go in building a relationship with his daughter. He forced a smile. "Genie is short for Genevieve, which is your full name. I think it's prettier than Genie, don't you?"

The child shrugged. "It's all right, I 'spose. Are you going to buy Mummy?"

The look he gave Zoe was blatantly assessing. "Are you for sale?"

"Of course not," Zoe denied furiously. Especially not to him. "You wouldn't want what I'm selling."

His interest notched upward visibly. "Don't be too sure."

Before she could respond, an announcement called them to the start of the auction and she had little choice but to tag along with James as he allowed himself to be towed toward the stage by an eager Genie. Zoe couldn't help noticing the admiring looks James garnered from the other women in the crowd, and even the occasional glance of envy from men who mistook the three of them for a family.

A large crowd had gathered to bid for the services on offer, especially as the money was for a good cause. Advertising space in the local newspaper raised a healthy sum as did supplies of meat and groceries. Dinner with the mayor was also popular as he was an agreeably good-looking bachelor.

Zoe braced herself for what she knew was coming. "Next we have a service, which should be popular. Ten hours of baby-sitting donated by our favorite local property gal, Zoe Holden. She's known as the best storyteller in the district, so who'll open the bidding at fifty dollars?"

Three bids in quick succession took the total to two hundred dollars before James raised his hand. "One thousand dollars."

There was a collective gasp and Zoe tugged at his arm. "You can't be serious."

"Never more so." He glanced at Genie. "It's a service I could well use."

Nothing like this had entered her mind when she donated her time to help the fund-raising effort. The thought of James having first claim on ten hours of her time sent a burst of heat flaring through her veins. In ten hours, they could— "No, I'll withdraw my donation," she said, hearing the alarm in her voice.

"Too late."

Not surprisingly James's bid attracted no opposition and the hammer fell with a resounding thud. "Sold to the gentleman with Zoe for one thousand dollars. Very generous of you, sir. We won't even ask what you intend to do with her for ten hours."

Laughter rippled through the crowd and Zoe felt herself color. They obviously thought James had bid for her out of chivalry. They couldn't be more wrong.

She endured a good deal more friendly teasing as James wrote out the check and handed it to the organizers. "Why did you do it?" she demanded when he returned to her side.

"It's for a good cause," he said mildly. "As I see it, I owe you more than I can possibly repay, and this is a small step toward balancing the books."

She recoiled instinctively. "You don't owe me anything." Nor did she care for the notion of James holding lease to her time.

He was unperturbed. "Then consider it simply a donation to the fund-raising effort." He regarded her keenly for a moment. "What would your price be, I wonder?"

"Only a cynic expects everyone to have a price," she tossed her answer back at him, uncomfortably aware that her price—if she had one—was the child now leaning sleepily against her legs. Did James sense that Genie was her price? How would he use the information? Andrew would have used it to get his own way, but James wasn't Andrew. What he would do she wasn't sure.

Genie yawned hugely, ending the discussion. "Time I got you home, sleepyhead," Zoe said, ruffling the fine dark hair, which felt like silk between her fingers.

James nodded agreement. "I'll drive you home. My car's not far away."

"We walked here. We can walk back," Zoe insisted.

He looked down at the child. "Genevieve's almost out on her feet. We'll take my car."

He led them to his car, which was parked beyond the closed-off section of the street. In the back was a brand-new child's booster seat. He had come well prepared, Zoe thought, fighting a sense of desolation as she watched him strap the child in. Pain sharpened her tongue. "Are you always this efficient?"

He slanted her a dry look. "If I was, my daughter wouldn't be in this position now."

So he blamed himself, at least in part, for Ruth's defection. Zoe stowed the discovery away for later examination as she slid into the front passenger seat. She wanted to ask what he planned to do next, but was too afraid of the possible answer. There was no doubt he had enjoyed spending this time with Genie. Zoe hadn't missed the way his absorbed expression had lighted on her every few minutes.

She sighed. Why couldn't Genie have chosen today to throw a world-class temper tantrum? "She isn't always as angelic as this," she observed.

His fingers tightened around the steering wheel. "As I shall probably find out for myself in time. Even if she'd been a little terror, it wouldn't make any difference. It doesn't to you.

"I see I've surprised you," he said, interpreting her silence with disturbing accuracy. "I may as well keep doing it by taking you and Genevieve out to dinner tonight."

Here at least she was on familiar ground. "You obviously don't know much about little girls. They spend the first half of the evening demanding food at once and the second half announcing that they're finished and can we please go home now."

A sheen of amusement filmed his eyes before he returned his attention to the road. The difference the smile made to his appearance made her catch her breath. For an instant he had looked not only human but so vulnerable that she could practically feel tiny cracks appearing in her resolve to keep him at a distance. Under different circumstances...

She reined in the errant thought. These circumstances were bad enough. She was unlikely to know him under any others. "So you see, a restaurant meal is a complete waste of time and money," she concluded.

"I might enjoy wasting both on my daughter," he said, stopping her in her tracks. "However," he went on, forestalling any more objections, "I defer to your experience in this at any rate. We can eat at home—yours or mine."

"Genie's too tired to go out again today," she demurred. She couldn't decide which was the more alarming prospect—going to his home or having him come to hers. "Frankly I'm tired too. Can't we do this another time?"

"Say, in another eighteen months? It isn't going to happen, Zoe, so we'll agree on dinner at your place. Don't worry about the catering. I'll take care of everything."

The quiet determination in his tone left no room for further discussion. She glanced at the child asleep in the back seat. "Then what will you do?"

"I'll let you know my plans at dinner tonight."

The mother in her rose like a tigress and she whipped sideways in her seat. "You can't mean to just take her away from me. She's only four and a half years old. She needs me." As much as I need her, she added but did not give it voice.

She might as well have appealed to solid granite for all the effect her words had on him. There was little mercy in the look he spared her, even for the tears that caught at the backs of her eyes, held in check by sheer willpower. She was not going to break down in front of him. Later would be time enough for tears, not now.

"Now you're getting a taste of what I've gone through for the last eighteen months," he stated.

"I've already had more than a taste," she said around a throat so tight it made speaking almost impossible. "Can you imagine how it felt to watch Genie grow every day, loving her more with every breath I took, yet knowing I couldn't adopt her? I was left to wonder with every knock on the door whether her family had been found and I would have to lose her.''

He hesitated for a heartbeat and hope welled within her so fast she felt as if it was a tidal wave crashing over her. Then he killed the hope. ''The knock on the door *has* come, Zoe. This evening you'll have to decide how you're going to deal with it.''

''If you were as heartless as this with Ruth, it's no wonder she ran away,'' Zoe said into the ragged silence that followed.

He gusted a long sigh. ''You can't hurt me with words, so it's pointless even to try. I'll be here at six this evening. Be ready.''

He parked the car outside her house, then came around to open the door and lifted Genie out of the back seat. The child drowsed with her head against his shoulder. He smoothed the tousled hair, the lines of his face softening as he gazed at Genie. ''Until tonight then.''

She took Genie from him, sensing his reluctance even as the child settled into her arms. ''Yes, tonight.''

The word resonated between them—part promise, part threat. Despite everything, she wished she had the courage to take Genie and disappear. Yet she knew she would be here when he called tonight.

Chapter Four

The evening ahead was also on James's mind as he threaded the turbo-charged car through impossible gaps in the afternoon traffic, taking a perverse pleasure in the progress he made.

The exercise reminded him of the motto on a boyhood money box: Tall Oaks From Little Acorns Grow. One car-length at a time eventually put you in front of the pack, just as eighteen months of searching yielded a daughter he could hardly wait to see again.

Lord, but she was beautiful. He grinned foolishly at himself in the rearview mirror as he pictured her tiny, perfectly formed fingers curled around his own. She'd been so pleased when he won the stuffed toy for her that he wished he could go back and do it again just to see the look on her face.

Was an adult capable of such unconditional love? A pain dragged at his heart as he thought about the last eighteen months. She had been a baby when he saw her last. Now she was a little girl. How could Ruth have robbed him of the miracle of watching her grow?

From Ruth his thoughts leapt to Zoe. Being around her disturbed him more than he wanted to admit, even to himself. It would have been simpler if she had been in league with Ruth somehow, so he could have aimed his pent-up anger and frustration at her. Now he knew she was as innocent in all of this as he was.

Unbidden, her image flashed into his mind. As soon as she opened her door to him he'd felt something powerful flash between them and he could swear she had felt it, too. Not that he intended to do anything about it. After his experience with Ruth he didn't need any more complications, especially of the female kind. The only woman he needed in his life right now was not yet five years old.

Yet his brain persisted in constructing a vision of Zoe in a snappy green dress that fit like crazy. Yet she wasn't beautiful in the usual sense. It was more a combination of features adding up to a thoroughly arresting effect. Like the way her hair fluffed out around her face in undisciplined curls, in a kind of halo. How would it feel to run his fingers through it? He'd bet anything it would be as soft as silk and smelling faintly of flowers.

She wasn't model-thin, either, but her hips were womanly and perfectly proportioned to the rest of her. Not a woman to get by on a lettuce leaf, he thought, grinning involuntarily, recalling the ice cream and hot dog she'd downed during their round of the street fair. He'd bet she had other strong appetites, too.

He pulled his thoughts up with a mental jerk. Her involvement with Genevieve was behind these strange fantasies. Apart from anything else, Zoe hated him for coming between her and the child she'd grown to love and, damn it, she had a right to. So why did he feel this grabbing sensation deep inside every time she looked at him? She hadn't even cared when Genevieve dripped ice cream on what was obviously an expensive dress, although he knew Ruth would have blown a gasket.

In short, Zoe Holden was nothing like Ruth—and it worried the heck out of him.

What was the absurd nickname she'd bestowed on his daughter? Genie. It would have to stop. He wasn't having his child sounding like something out of a magic lamp.

Zoe would probably find a way to shorten her own name if she could. Zoe. He played with the name in his mind. It sounded a bit like zowee, a crazy word he and his sister had used as children to describe anything really terrific. Funny, he hadn't given the word a thought in years.

He braked impatiently as a delivery van cut in ahead of him. Now was hardly the time to indulge in flights of fantasy. He had a new and challenging role ahead of him, which he intended to tackle with the same zeal usually applied to business.

Remembering his doctor's advice, he decided to start right away.

Picking up the voice-activated recorder he always carried with him, he began dictating a memo to his secretary, Angela. "I want you to have Brian take over for me for the next few weeks. I can be contacted at White Stars in emergency but don't expect me in the office for a while." He grinned, picturing Angela's reaction to his next words. "You'll be pleased to know your boss is finally taking that vacation you've been nagging me about."

He wasn't concerned about taking the break. Angela ran his office like a well-oiled machine. She knew what she could safely handle in his absence and what should be referred to himself or to Brian, his deputy. He was glad now that he had anticipated such an eventuality. Too many companies depended on one man and foundered if that man glanced away. James didn't intend his company to be among them.

He lifted the recorder. "I'm also turning over the purchase of the Strathfield mansion to Brian. The paperwork is already on its way to you from the agent, Zoe Holden." He knew his secretary well enough to add, "And you can take those stars out of your eyes, Ms. Davis. I'm not going off to play house with Zoe Holden. Just because you're engaged to be married doesn't mean the rest of the world floats on a cloud of romance."

He added several business notes before ending the tape, which he planned to drop off on his way past the office. Then he'd officially be on leave. He started to whistle and actually let several chances to switch lanes pass him by, feeling lighter and more carefree than he had in a long time.

Was he so uplifted by the idea of a vacation? Hardly. He didn't find recreation especially relaxing, except for the exhilaration of riding one of his prize Arabian horses at White Stars. And after his doctor's stern injunction to take things easy, he guessed horse riding was out for a while. So what, then?

He refused to attribute his elevated mood to Zoe Holden, however much his starry-eyed secretary might wish it to be so. For a start, Zoe was a blonde and they had never turned him on.

Well, maybe not blond exactly. What would he call the elusive color of her hair, which flowed around her shoulders like handfuls of silk? Palomino? It had a unique honey sheen with platinum highlights, much too unusual to be merely blond. And judging from the way she'd guarded Genevieve like a tigress protecting its cub, she had an inner strength to match. He had a feeling that separating her from his child was going to be more of a challenge than the eighteen months of searching put together.

Zoe flashed her neighbor an apologetic smile. "I hope Simon isn't too disappointed about missing our video date tonight."

Julie shook her head. "My sister is coming over with her twins. They're a year younger than Simon and he loves bossing them around." She added milk to the mug of coffee Zoe put in front of her. "Besides, reruns of *Bambi* can't compare with dinner with a gorgeous hunk like James Langford."

Zoe took a deep breath. "It isn't what you think, Julie. He's a client, nothing more."

Julie regarded her keenly. "Since when does a client bring such a flush to your cheeks. Not that it's a bad thing. Andrew burned you badly, but it doesn't mean all men are the same."

Zoe sighed. "I know, but I'm not ready to risk it again, even so." And especially not with a man like James Langford. If they had met under other circumstances, things might have been different. But he was Genie's father first and foremost, and Zoe was simply an obstacle in his way. Added to which, his willingness to have her investigated without her knowledge reminded her much too uncomfortably of Andrew's despicable behavior.

So why did her emotions threaten to overwhelm her every time she thought of James? He struck a chord of longing deep inside her, she recognized, reminding her of needs she had barely allowed herself to own in over two years.

She became aware that Julie was watching her intently. "What's really going on here, Zoe?"

"Nothing. Why do you ask?"

"We've been friends for too long." Her eyes widened with concern. "Is it something to do with Genie?"

Zoe felt her eyes brim and the tightness in her chest increased. "Oh, Julie, I don't know what I'm going to do. James is Genie's real father."

Coffee spilled from her friend's cup as she recoiled in

astonishment. "Her father? No wonder you look as if your world has ended. When did you find out?"

"James came on the pretext of inspecting the Strathfield place, while you and the kids were at playgroup."

Julie gave a soundless whistle. "You had no idea what he really wanted?"

Zoe shook her head. "I thought it was strictly business until he showed me the documentation. There's no doubt."

"This is really rough on you," Julie said in concern. "If there's anything I can do to help..."

"Thanks, but there isn't much anyone can do. My only hope is to make him understand that Genie needs me as much as she needs a father."

Julie looked aghast. "He can't mean to take her away from you completely?"

"It's possible." Zoe lifted pain-filled eyes to her friend. "He has the law on his side. The crazy part is, I don't even blame him. I hate what he's doing to me, but in his place I'd do exactly the same thing."

Julie's eyes narrowed. "There's more to this, though, isn't there?"

Zoe looked away. "You're imagining things."

"No, I'm not. You're attracted to him, aren't you?"

Zoe's jerking movement upset her coffee and hot liquid flowed across the countertop. Mopping it up enabled her to avert her flushed face from Julie's searching appraisal. "Clumsy of me," she muttered. "It must be all the stress."

Julie was not to be sidetracked. "It could also be that I'm on the right track."

"You can't be. He's the man who intends to take my child away. I may never see her again, and certainly not as her mother. How can I possibly feel attracted to him?"

Julie shrugged. "Who says we're only attracted to suitable men? Neither of my husbands was what you'd call suitable. Neither was Andrew, come to mention it, but we married them anyway. Chemistry is the darnedest thing, sometimes impossible to resist.''

Zoe nodded. ''You're right as usual. I was naive enough to mistake Andrew's jealousy as proof of his love. I don't plan on making such a fool of myself again, especially not with a man who thinks I'm in his way.''

Julie folded her arms across her chest. ''Admitting you find him attractive doesn't mean you're being disloyal to Genie, you know. It could be the perfect solution, if the two most important people in her life got together.''

The very idea sent a shiver down Zoe's spine. Julie hadn't met James or seen the determination in his eyes when he vowed to take Genie back. He wasn't likely to let anything stand in his way, even any feelings he might have for Zoe. She clamped her hands over her ears. ''Stop it. James isn't interested in me. I'm only an obstacle to get to his daughter.''

''Not an enviable position to be in if everything I've heard about him is true,'' Julie observed. ''*World Magazine* said he made his first million at twenty and doesn't have anything to do with his family. And something must have been wrong for his wife to run away and take his child. Did he tell you what happened?''

Briefly Zoe explained about James's marriage. ''It seems his wife was the one with the problem,'' she concluded.

''But there are two sides to every argument. Maybe he's a closet sadist who beats women,'' Julie speculated.

Zoe shook her head. ''He may be single-minded and ruthless in business, but he doesn't seem cruel.''

''You said he returned to the Middle East after Genie was born. Maybe he runs a harem over there,'' Julie persisted.

Knowing the way James had stirred her own blood, Zoe allowed that Julie's screwball theory was closer to being possible. Not a harem, but perhaps an affair, which Ruth had discovered. Maybe it was James and not Ruth who had chafed against the strictures of married life. To Zoe's surprise she found she didn't really want to believe it.

"This is getting me nowhere," she said finally. "No matter how attractive James is—and yes, I agree he is—he is still the enemy."

"Sorry to play devil's advocate, but I gather you don't think Genie would be better off with him?"

Zoe chewed her lower lip thoughtfully. "He may be her biological father, but if he was too caught up in his own affairs to come back to his wife and child, how long will it be before the novelty of fatherhood wears off again?"

"What are you going to do?"

Zoe squared her shoulders. "Somehow I have to convince him that Genie needs me. If I can't, maybe there's a legal avenue I can try."

Julie looked distressed. "So much for my notion of a romantic dinner *à deux*. It sounds more like meat cleavers at ten paces. Do you want me to stay as backup?"

Zoe shook her head. "Enjoy your evening with your sister. I can handle James Langford."

Brave words, she thought as she tidied away the coffee things after Julie and her young son had gone home. In spite of her assurances to her friend, Zoe wasn't at all sure she could live up to them.

The trouble was, as she'd confessed to Julie, she did understand how James felt. Her own love for Genie was so strong she could easily imagine the torment of having the little girl hidden from her. It was every parent's worst nightmare. Maybe it was why she felt so drawn to James. Somehow it was hard to make herself believe it.

The house seemed preternaturally still, almost like a promise of things to come. She found herself looking in on

Genie every few minutes, to reassure herself the little girl was still happily engrossed with her dolls.

Suddenly Zoe straightened. She was acting as if James had already won. She was letting herself get used to the idea of life without Genie. Maybe James *had* won. Maybe she could do nothing to change the outcome. But maybe she could. Surely she owed it to her daughter not to give up? Genie's very presence in her life was a miracle. If it took another one to keep her, Zoe would simply have to find one.

Chapter Five

Despite her resolution, she was far from prepared when James arrived that evening. Even less so when she opened the door to find him holding an enormous bouquet of perfect yellow roses. Their perfume enveloped her in a sensuous cloud, which made her head spin.

It had nothing to do with the sight of James on her doorstep, she told herself determinedly. All the same she was vividly aware of a mass of small details such as the way the porch light glinted off his dark hair, highlighting the masculine waves that strayed across his high, intelligent forehead.

Her fingers didn't really itch to smooth the hair out of his eyes, she thought, clenching her fingers in automatic self-defense. James was well prepared to use his natural advantages to achieve his purposes. That she was already reacting to him on a physical level should be warning enough of the threat he represented to her well-being.

"Come in," she invited in a voice less than steady.

"For you." He offered the roses. Only someone as

self-assured as James could carry the flowers and still look unreservedly masculine, she thought, uncomfortably aware of her heart picking up speed.

Deliberately she placed the bouquet on the hall table, stressing their unimportance, although every fiber of her being urged her to cherish the magnificent flowers because they were a gift from him. All the more reason to let him think they were of no importance to her, she told herself. That he was of no importance to her. No other possibility was acceptable.

He passed the flowers without comment. As she went to close the door, he said, "Anton is right behind me with our dinner."

"You meant it when you said you'd take care of everything." In a kind of defiance against what she was feeling toward him, she'd refused to plan anything for the evening. If it meant he ate nothing, so be it. She wasn't about to spend hours in the kitchen cooking for a man who meant to destroy her life.

His direct gaze jolted through her as he said, "I always mean what I say."

Refusing to consider the possibilities this opened up, she struggled to frame a reply. They were interrupted by a black-bearded bear of a man in chef's garb, his arms laden with provisions. After a brief greeting and request for directions, Chef Anton aimed himself at her kitchen from which soon emanated the sounds of food being prepared.

Zoe had a sense of being run over by a steamroller, or was it the Aussie Bulldozer? "I didn't realize you meant to bring your chef to make dinner here," she snapped.

His eyebrow lifted. "Does it matter? We have more pressing matters to discuss."

"Now that you've established your superior status." Having his chef here reminded her uncomfortably of James's power, his ability to move people around like chess pieces. Had Ruth also objected to being a pawn in his game?

He paused in the act of uncorking a bottle of vintage Chardonnay. "It never occurred to me to check with you. Anton is here for your convenience as much as mine."

He couldn't understand her objection, she thought in consternation. "All the same, it does emphasize the difference in our life-styles."

He held out a brimming glass. "I don't intend to use my financial status as a bargaining chip. This isn't about who can give Genevieve the most toys. What matters is what's best for her welfare."

Zoe accepted the glass but didn't drink. The glass felt icy in her fevered grasp. "Even if it's to leave her in my care?"

"If it was best for her, that's precisely what I would do."

"But you don't believe it is."

His expression hardened. "She belongs with her family, Zoe."

She spread her hands beseechingly. "Are you certain you're the best person to take care of her? Materially you can give her more than I ever can, but what about other more important considerations?" Such as a mother's love, she added silently.

He looked as if he was tempted to debate the issue with her, then decided against it and set his glass down. "I'd like to see her now."

"She's playing in her room," she said, suddenly hoarse.

As she moved to lead the way, he placed a hand on her arm. "Just tell me which way."

His touch created instant havoc inside her. Her heart began to pound and her tongue stuck to the roof of her mouth. His hand felt fiery on her arm, his nearness creating a searing awareness like a hunger. It was over in a flash, but its passing left her shaken. What was going on here? He was the enemy, the man who would take her child. Yet at some level she knew her response had nothing to do with Genie.

"Which way?" he prompted again. The spell shattered and she could function again, but barely. She moved woodenly toward the hallway and gestured to a half-open door. He nodded, his breathing as much of an effort as hers, as he pushed the door all the way open. Genie sat on the floor surrounded by her family of dolls.

Zoe held her breath as James dropped to his knees to put himself on Genie's level. "Hello, sweetheart. Recovered from the excitement of the fair?"

After a quick glance at Zoe for reassurance, Genie smiled back. "Hi, James. Woof is saying hello to my dolls."

Woof was the newly christened toy dog James had won for her at the fair. It had quickly been absorbed into Genie's make-believe family. Urged on by James, Genie began to introduce her toys to him.

The scene took only moments, but Zoe could hardly believe the transformation. From initial uncertainty, Genie had relaxed into complete acceptance of James, taking her cue from his gentle tone and genuine interest in her game.

Zoe's thoughts spun. Was this the man whose presence in her house set her heart thudding so hard it felt as if someone was playing drumbeats on her chest? Where was the corporate warrior now, down on his knees with a four-year-old? She was reminded of Ruth's description of him as ruthless and insensitive. If he was, he concealed it amazingly well.

James got to his feet, heedless of his impeccably tailored trousers, and offered Genie his hand. "Ready for some dinner?"

"I already had mine," Genie said importantly. "I had fish fingers and mashed potato mountains."

"Then you don't mind if I have dinner with Zoe?" he asked the child.

She shook her head. "Can I have some ice cream?"

He glanced at Zoe who nodded. "She usually eats earlier, but sometimes I let her have dessert later as a treat."

"Then I'll have the chef make you some ice cream," he promised.

Genie cocked her head to one side. "What's a chef?"

"It's a person who cooks for other people," he explained, sounding slightly bemused.

"That's a funny name for a mummy."

His glance flickered to Zoe, his interest aroused. "What else do mummies do besides cook dinner?"

Genie looked scornful, as if his ignorance was beyond belief. "They do lots of things. Put bandages on hurts, help at playgroup and show nice men houses."

"Do they indeed?"

Genie nodded. "Auntie Julie took me and Simon to playgroup because Mummy had to show a nice man a house."

Zoe's heart sank. In her innocence Genie had confirmed James's suspicion that Zoe put her work first and her child second.

But he only said, "Guess what? I'm the man your mummy showed the house to."

Genie inspected his dark suit and tie gravely. "Mummy said he lives in the country. Do you live in the country?"

He nodded solemnly. "Where I live you can ride for hours and still be on my land."

The child's eyes went as round as saucers. "You mean ride real live horses?"

Something shattered inside Zoe. Unwittingly James had mentioned the one subject dearest to Genie's heart. She was horse crazy. Even her Barbie dolls had their own horse who was cared for as carefully as a real one.

On a visit to the Royal Easter Show last year, the horses had been Genie's sole interest. Other children had spent their pocket money on show bags filled with sweets and toys. Genie came home smelling of hay and horses, her expression blissful. She wore the same look of transcendence now as James pulled some photos out of his wallet. From where she stood, Zoe saw they were pictures of Arabian horses. How could Fate have given James such an unfair advantage?

It was hard enough to endure the sight of James and Genie so close together, two sleek dark heads almost touching. Zoe had always known Genie's coloring didn't come from Ruth. Now the source was all too apparent, as was the rapport between them as they looked at the photographs.

Zoe levered herself upright against the door frame. Keep putting one foot in front of the other, she instructed herself. This was only a slight setback. "Thank James for showing you the photos," she instructed, proud that the tremors racking her didn't show in her voice.

"Thank you, James," Genie said obediently, but her dejected posture tore at Zoe's heartstrings.

James's jaw set. "How would you like to visit my horses, Genevieve?"

The ground shifted beneath Zoe's feet. No, he couldn't do this to her. But the change in Genie's expression from downcast to radiant showed how successfully he *had*. "Can I? Really? When?"

He smiled. "Soon. I promise." He offered the child his hand. "How about that ice cream now?"

So this was how Zoe's world would end. Genie's fingers looked so small curled in his powerful ones. The child herself looked breathtakingly tiny beside her tall, wide-shouldered father. Yet there was no denying the resemblance between them. Genie looked so right at his side that Zoe almost choked on the lump filling her throat. Even without the documents James had brought with him, she would have been forced to accept that Genie was his daughter.

She managed to smile as James seated her, then Genie, at the dining table, which the chef had set in their absence. At any other time she would have enjoyed being spoiled. Gleaming silverware and delicate china glowed in the mellow light of candles, and appetizing aromas wafted from serving dishes in the center of the table. It would be so easy to sink into fantasy and imagine them as one happy family. But nothing was further from the truth.

"I told Anton we'll serve ourselves," James said. Deftly he transferred fresh Sydney Rock oysters to her plate, the seafood garnished with roast shallot and basil vinaigrette. It was accompanied by a glistening Caesar salad, but her throat closed around the first mouthful she tried to swallow. She settled for pushing the food around on her plate.

Genie had no such problem. At James's request Anton had produced a lavish strawberry parfait for her. "All for me?" the child said, wide-eyed, when it was set in front of her.

"All for you," James agreed, smiling at her reaction. "I'll make sure there's ice cream on the menu every night when you come to White Stars."

Zoe's insides cramped in protest as Genie asked, "What's White Stars?"

From long-ago school poetry lessons, Zoe recalled a Banjo Paterson poem about air as clear as crystal where white stars fairly blazed. It must be the name of his horse stud.

She was right. "It's my home in the country, where my Arabian horses live. I want you to see it."

"But not for a while," Zoe countered. It was much too soon. Genie wasn't ready. Zoe wasn't ready, if the truth be told.

James's face darkened. "Why not? Genevieve doesn't start school for months. It's the ideal time."

"Can we, Mummy? James has real horses."

Zoe wanted to kill him. How could she compete with a country property and real horses? "It's your bedtime, Genie," she announced, trying to mask her distress. "James and I will talk about a visit and see what can be arranged."

"Yippee." For Genie the decision was all but made. Zoe wanted to cry. James had said that Genie's future wasn't about who offered the most toys, but wasn't this bribery of the worst kind?

Settling Genie down to sleep was almost impossible. By the time Zoe returned to the table, she was fuming. "What do you think you're doing?" she demanded, hands on hips, eyes blazing.

"Pleasing my daughter," he said, her fury rolling off him.

She slumped into her chair again. "Bribing her, you mean. Trying to win her over with ponies and a property where she can only be in your way."

His look was startlingly direct. "She won't be in my way. I've rearranged my business affairs so I can be with her at White Stars for the next few weeks."

Appalled, she stared at him. "Few weeks? You've got it all planned, haven't you?"

He rested his forearms on the table, meeting her angry gaze levelly. "Hoping isn't the same as planning. I hoped it would work out like this. Can you think of a better way for me to get to know my daughter?" She couldn't and he knew it. He nodded as if she'd agreed. "Of course, I'll understand if you choose not to come with us."

A tight fist closed around her heart. "You mean you hope I won't."

"Believe it or not, I hope you will. You can see for

yourself how keen Genevieve is to go. It will make things easier if you're there, at least at the start."

Her heart sank. He must know she couldn't refuse to make the transition as easy as possible for Genie, no matter how much it cost her personally. "You win. We'll go to White Stars," she said tiredly. "But it's only for a holiday. If Genie is the least bit unhappy—"

"I'll bring her back to Sydney myself."

It was as much as Zoe could hope for. "I suppose you're happy now that you've got what you wanted."

"If I'd gotten what I wanted, Genevieve and I would be on our way to White Stars right now."

"Instead you're stuck with me."

After a long pause, he said, "Have you thought I might consider it a pleasure?"

Look up, meet his eyes or you never will, she commanded herself. Heat tore through her veins and it took all her resolve to say, "Pleasure is hardly the word I'd use."

A flush seared her face as he began a feature-by-feature assessment. Warmth seemed to follow the path of his gaze, but she made herself meet his scrutiny without wavering. "Maybe not yet," he said finally, the deep baritone of his voice washing over her like a caress.

"Not ever," she said, recognizing the shakiness of the denial. She was fairly sure he heard it, too.

He pushed his chair back from the table and came around to pull her chair out for her. As she stood up, she collided with the hard wall of his chest. Shock and something unfathomable rioted through her. Desire? It was impossible, surely?

In the instant she stood within the circle of his arms, she felt the embers of passion kindle into flames. In another minute he would kiss her. She knew it as surely as she knew her own name. And she wouldn't do a thing to stop him.

* * *

James was stunned by the avalanche of emotions pouring through him. His shoulders ached with the effort of keeping his arms at his sides. It would be so easy to wrap them around Zoe and pull her hard against him.

He hadn't felt anything this powerful since his courting days in the Middle East, and a lot of that could be blamed on the isolation and political tensions of the time. What could he blame this on?

He swung around, but not before he glimpsed a look in Zoe's eyes he could swear was disappointment. Had she wanted him to give in to his instincts and kiss her? Ruth had used sex to get her own way, assuring him that all women were the same. If it was true, then Zoe knew the effect she had on him and somehow hoped to use it to change his mind about taking Genevieve.

Her next words dispelled some of this notion. "I hope you don't think you can charm me out of doing the right thing by Genie."

He almost laughed. She was accusing *him* of using sex as a bargaining chip. "Then you admit I could charm you?" he couldn't resist asking. Somehow the idea was more pleasing than it should have been.

She affected a none-too-convincing shrug. "You're the last man on earth to interest me in that way."

It came to him that she certainly interested him in that way, but instinct warned him against saying so. There would be time enough to explore such possibilities when they got to his property. "Then it's just as well that White Stars has a full staff, so you won't want for chaperones."

He had trouble believing his own ears. Why was he trying so hard to reassure her about the visit? It would be simpler to convince her to remain behind. The break from Genevieve would have to come sooner or later.

Against all logic he wanted Zoe to come to White Stars,

the only real home he'd known in his adult life. He wanted her to share his enthusiasm for the magnificent Arabian horses roaming the valleys, and for the secret rain forest retreats he'd found on his rambles.

He tried to tell himself it was for Genevieve's sake. Once Zoe saw for herself what a paradise White Stars was for a child, she would be less resistant to his plans. They included moving his base of operations permanently to the property so he could provide a secure home for Genevieve. But he knew it was only part of the reason he wanted Zoe there. The other part was much more down to earth and far less laudable. He wanted Zoe, period.

Chapter Six

"How about a swim this morning?" Zoe asked Genie. It was hard to believe they'd been at White Stars for over a week and hadn't tried out the magnificently landscaped pool. Back home in Sydney, Genie was a real water-baby, eager to practice her babyish swimming skills every chance she got.

So Zoe was surprised to see the child's face fall. "Do I have to? Grace is giving me a riding lesson today."

Grace McGovern was the capable woman James employed as stud manager. Her husband, Jock, also worked for James and the couple lived in one of the many buildings, which made up the homestead complex. "You've had a riding lesson practically every day since we got here. You mustn't monopolize Grace's time when she has a lot of work to do."

Genie stuck out her chin. "I don't mopolize her. James says I can ride anytime I want and Grace will look after me."

Zoe's spirits tumbled. James says. James says. It seems

she heard little else lately. "All the same, I'm sure he doesn't mean you to take up so much of Grace's time."

"Yes, he does."

Her reaction to the deep baritone intrusion shocked her with its intensity. A tingle ran down her spine and her heart began to thump in sympathetic cadence. She had hoped a week under his roof would somehow lessen his effect on her, but instead it had increased until he only needed to walk into the same room to set her senses on automatic alert.

She took refuge in annoyance. "Can we discuss this privately?"

His vivid eyes bored into her as if he was well aware of her reaction. "Yes, but it won't change the facts. I instructed Grace to give Genevieve's needs priority."

"Until when?"

"Until I tell her differently."

He ushered Genie outside to where Grace waited with a pony on a lunge rein to begin the lesson. Watching them through a picture window, Zoe's stomach clenched in protest. Slowly but surely Genie was slipping away from her, seduced by ponies, riding gear and beautiful possessions, far more than Zoe could have provided. How long before the child transferred all her affection to James?

Telling herself it was his due as Genie's father didn't make it any easier to endure. Zoe felt as if her heart was being ripped out, piece by little piece.

James on the other hand looked composed when he came back into the room. "You have a problem with Genevieve learning to ride?"

"I have a problem with your idea of child rearing," she snapped back, her anger driven as much by her infuriating response to him as by his obvious spoiling of Genie. "You may win her over, but you'll ruin a beautiful child."

A muscle tightened in his jaw. "Riding lessons won't

ruin her. Grace has raised four children. She doesn't let Genevieve get all her own way. Why don't you relax and enjoy the break.''

Her control was perilously close to snapping. "Don't patronize me. I didn't come to White Stars for a holiday. I came to be with Genie.''

"Was it your only reason?''

The question was so unexpected that she was unable to prevent her face from betraying her. Try as she might to deny it, spending time with James at White Stars had appealed to her. She hadn't forgotten the impact of her first sight of him on her doorstep, so magnificently male, so ruggedly attractive. Discovering his hidden agenda had devastated her, but it hadn't diminished the forbidden-fruit aura he projected. Was she a masochist? First Andrew with his jealous possessiveness, now James whose aim was to remove her from Genie's life as swiftly as possible.

She felt the color settle high on her cheeks. "It's the only reason that matters.''

He moved closer and her breathing quickened automatically, but he remained behind her, a heartbeat away. "I know how rough this is for you, Zoe.''

She could handle almost anything but his pity. Her eyes swam and she blinked furiously. "I'm fine, really. It's just—everything's happening so fast.'' One minute she was in Sydney with Genie, the next she was on extended leave from her job, Julie was keeping an eye on her house and she was living at White Stars trying to prepare herself for a future without her child.

He was so close now that if she leaned back a little, his arms would come around her, and she would be cradled against his broad chest. The memory of his mouth against her skin made a second taste even more imperative. She actually licked her lips in anticipation.

"It can't happen too fast for me,'' he stated.

Reason returned with a rush as his words slammed into her. He was determined to take Genie from her as expeditiously as possible, even if it meant making love to her to achieve it.

Nevertheless, stiffening her spine enough to step away from him took courage. Lifting her head high so he wouldn't see the effort it cost her, she headed outside to the training paddock.

Watching her go, James felt physically drained, recognizing the start of a headache that would soon be pounding in his temples. He unclenched his fists and took deep breaths, trying to hold the pain at bay. Zoe didn't know why he couldn't afford to take this slowly or be as considerate of her feelings as he might have been. But he didn't have the luxury of a choice. He needed to get Genevieve settled at White Stars as quickly as possible.

Bill Margolin had made it clear the operation couldn't be postponed for much longer. James had intended to bring Genevieve here, then make whatever arrangements the doctor advised. But after seeing his child again, he'd gotten greedy. Now he wanted to spend as much time as he could with her before submitting to the knife that would either cure—or kill—him.

Then there was Zoe of the flashing eyes and tumbling palomino curls and a stubbornness to equal his own. He had never wanted a future as badly as he did since meeting her, to explore what they could be to each other. Hell, to explore her beautiful, sexy body for glorious nights on end. The need was so strong it was like fire in his blood.

Forget it, pal, it can't happen, he told himself. To her he was the enemy and he would need time to change her mind, the one thing he didn't have. Better to count his blessings in finding Genevieve and wish Zoe a great life with a man whose chances of survival were better than fifty-fifty.

Damn, but his head hurt.

At some level he knew the pain was caused by more than the bullet pressing against a nerve in his spine. It had a lot to do with imagining Zoe in the arms of another man.

Zoe's mouth dried as she watched Grace guide Genie's horse around the training paddock on the end of a long lunge rein. Despite James's assurance that Genie's mount, a gray Arabian pony called White Stars Amira, was quiet and well mannered, the horse looked alarmingly powerful in contrast to the tiny, inexperienced rider.

James assured her the Arabian horses were gentle and affectionate despite their spirited looks. Like her rider, Amira was a four-year-old with the elegant profile, flaring nostrils and small muzzle of her breed, her pedigree showing in her gracefully arched neck, long, sloping shoulders and broad chest.

Genie was unconcerned by pedigrees. To her a horse was a horse, to be loved, petted and hugged without reservation. The child had absolutely no fear even of James's magnificent black stallion, Ferrere.

At the moment Genie was learning to balance, riding with her arms outstretched at her sides and her feet free of the stirrups. With her sweet face screwed up in intense concentration, she looked the picture of happiness.

Suddenly a shriek tore the air. In horror Zoe watched Genie begin to slip sideways, grabbing futilely at the horse's mane as she lost her balance. Zoe was impossibly far away with no way to prevent what was happening.

She went cold from head to foot as Genie lost her precarious grip on the horse's mane and pitched toward the ground. Instinctively Zoe threw herself between the lower rungs of the whitewashed railings, but was pulled back by strong masculine arms. She flailed in James's grasp. "What are you doing? Let me go to her."

"It's all right. Grace has everything under control."

"But Genie fell. She may be hurt."

Her struggles were useless against his iron grip. "She isn't hurt. Look."

Terrified of what she would see, Zoe made herself look across the paddock. She sagged in James's grip as Grace helped Genie to her feet, checked her over and dusted her off. The child even giggled as she was lifted back into the saddle. "You can't mean to let her ride again after such a bad fall."

"Try and stop her," he said wryly. "She's having the time of her life. If you rush over there now, you'll only transmit your fear to her. You don't want that, do you?"

"What I want is to protect my baby," she said, amazed to find she could actually speak through clenched teeth.

His eyes betrayed no flicker of emotion, but the lines around his mouth tightened. "In the first place, she isn't a baby and in the second, she doesn't need protecting. Riding comes as naturally to her as breathing."

"I see you want to believe it." How could he care anything for Genie if he was prepared to put her at such risk? "Isn't it enough to have a daughter without forcing her to fit your mold as well?"

His face darkened. "Nobody's trying to mold her. She loves what she's doing."

"You've made sure of it, haven't you, by pandering to her every whim. I've hardly seen her since we arrived. It's all part of your plan, isn't it?"

The warning signs in his eyes intensified. "You don't know what you're talking about."

She ignored the warnings and plunged on, the shock of Genie's near-miss fueling her anger. "Don't I? Next you'll have her calling you boss like everyone else around here."

"It will be her choice. She has to call me something."

"But you won't exactly discourage it, will you?"

His eyes narrowed. "What would you suggest she call me? Personally I prefer Daddy."

Zoe tossed her head, her response to him at odds with her urge to protect Genie. "She's too young for what I'd suggest she call you. I thought you wanted to get to know her, not alienate her from me completely."

He still held her arm as he began to tow her toward the stables complex. "This isn't the place to discuss it."

She dug her heels into the velvet turf but might as well have tried to restrain a raging bull for all the good it did her. "I'm not moving from here until Genie's safely off that horse," she said futilely as James continued to steer her toward the stables.

"Which is precisely why you're coming with me. Would you rather walk or be carried?"

He was perfectly capable of it, she thought, as an image of herself in his arms invaded her mind. No point in challenging him unless she was prepared for the consequences. Already the touch of his hand generated an internal heat she found thoroughly disconcerting. It was pure chemistry, borne out of her emotionally fragile state, but the conviction didn't lessen the intensity. "I can walk, thank you," she said stiffly, releasing a strangled breath when he finally let go of her arm.

His breathing was less than steady, she noted. James must feel the electricity that flashed between them every time he touched her. It must be highly inconvenient for him, if so. She was sure that consorting with the enemy wasn't high on his agenda, either.

In simmering silence she walked beside him toward the stables complex, past rows of immaculate stalls, which smelled sweetly of hay and pampered horseflesh, to a suite of offices on a mezzanine floor.

She might have known his office would be the largest and most luxurious. State-of-the-art computer equipment and a video-telephone cluttered an enormous lime washed oak desk while the other half of the spacious room held two butter-colored leather sofas and a glass coffee table. Beyond them a wall of glass framed a view of the rolling hills and paddocks as if they were living works of art.

He steered her to one of the sofas and she dropped gracelessly onto it. "Drink?" he asked.

"No, thank you." If he thought he could turn this into a social visit and somehow charm her into agreeing with his plans for Genie, he was out of luck. "Say what you dragged me in here to say and let me get back to the training paddock."

"Genevieve doesn't need you watching her every move. Why do you think she took a tumble?"

Zoe felt a slow burn rising. "You think the fall was my fault?"

"You're a distraction. If I felt your fear from where I stood, imagine its effect on a small child."

He was too much. "Now I'm a distraction. I'm surprised you don't ship me back to Sydney and be done with it. Why did you invite me here if you intended to drive a wedge between me and Genie all along?"

"Isn't it what you're trying to do to me? No matter what I want to do for her, you fight me at every turn."

"I only want what's best for her," she insisted, her voice dropping to a strangled whisper.

"Well at least we agree on something," he said, an edge like a knife in his tone. He braced his palms against his hips. "Despite what you think of me, I'm not a monster. All I want is the right to be a father to my own child, a right denied to me for almost two years."

He began to pace, his long legs eating up the floor space. Each circuit brought him a little closer until her breathing constricted. He reminded her of a jungle animal prowling his domain. Watching him, Zoe was reminded of the ancient Greek belief that panthers snared prey by casting a spell over them, the panther's scent becoming associated with magic and seduction. She saw both in every line of his lithe movements and she felt as mesmerized as any prey.

It was an effort to drag her eyes away. "Punishing me by keeping us apart won't change what you've gone through."

His thunderous look impaled her. "You may see this as punishment, but it isn't my doing. It's Genevieve's choice to spend every moment she can at the stables. Grace tells me she would sleep there if she could, to be near her beloved horses."

There was no arguing this truth. "Then it isn't some kind of plot to separate me from her?"

"Of course not."

He was almost beside her now, his commanding figure blotting out her view of the ridges and valleys beyond the windows. Blotting out a lot of things, such as her ability to think straight. Her thoughts whirled. She tried thinking of Genie, reminding herself that James was the one coming between them. It did little good. Her mind seemed fixated on one thing only—how much of a man he was.

Aspects of him that she'd been trying to ignore forced themselves into her consciousness. The muscular build that would have inspired Michelangelo. The way his chestnut hair was cut in thick rising waves with square-cut sideburns that practically invited her to run her fingers through it. In that moment his eyes locked with hers, and she felt as if all resistance was being drained from her.

He knew precisely what effect he was having on her, she saw with terrifying certainty. He knew when it was the last thing she wanted him to know, or to feel for that matter. He was the enemy. Being attracted to him was no more on her agenda than it must be on his.

He came closer and she stood up, the better to meet him on his own level. Or as near as she could manage when her head barely reached past his shoulder. She was braced for an argument, not for his arms to come around her. The suddenness of his movement took her breath away, and she found herself leaning into the embrace when common sense dictated the very opposite.

His lips on hers triggered an inner dilemma. Fight or flight? One or the other seemed advisable. Anything but surrender. Yet surrender was perilously close as he kissed her throat, her earlobes and the sensitive nape of her neck. She seemed incapable of doing anything else as he awakened needs she hadn't allowed herself to acknowledge for a long time. Her breath escaped in a ragged sigh as she tilted her head back, her eyes closing almost of their own accord.

Magic and seduction were the panther's stock-in-trade, she reminded herself dazedly. Both infused his embrace, yet she couldn't quite make herself believe she had no choice in this. Somehow she knew all she had to do was push him away, however halfheartedly, and he would stop instantly. So why didn't she? What on earth possessed her to link her arms around his neck and pull his head down to her?

She felt as if she was being set on fire, consumed by flames of desire so powerful they burned away all reason. Her throat felt too raw to draw a whole breath, and her limbs turned leaden and languorous. James ran a hand down the length of her spine and she shuddered deliciously.

"You see, there's no need for war between us when we can have so much more," he said throatily. "If we'd met under normal circumstances, we may have been lovers by now."

But they hadn't met in the normal way. And there was a need for war between them until Genie's future was worked out. Was this James's way of persuading Zoe to accept his plans for the child? She forced herself to look up at him. "This isn't going to work."

Mild amusement flickered in the softly upturned set of his sensuous mouth. "What isn't going to work?"

She slid out of the circle of his arms, aware that part of her still wanted all that James represented. But she steeled herself not to give in to it. The price was simply too high. "This…this scheme of yours to get me to do what you want."

"A moment ago it was what you wanted, too." His voice sounded as throaty as hers felt.

The truth couldn't be denied. She *had* wanted him to kiss her. For all their differences, she sensed he wasn't the sort of man to force himself on a woman. He had no need to, she acknowledged shakily. His wealth and power weren't the source of his magnetic appeal as much as his unbridled masculinity. Her mistake was in misjudging his effect on her, which had almost distracted her from the real reason she was here—for Genie.

She felt a flush rising. "I admit I did want it, but that was before I realized what you were doing."

He crossed his arms over his broad chest. "Okay, I'll bite. What was I doing?"

"Making love to me so I'll stop resisting your plans. You said yourself it couldn't happen too fast for you."

His face remained level, but his eyes held a fire that made her catch her breath. "You underestimate yourself, Zoe."

She didn't want to consider that possibility, but heat invaded her face, among other places. The atmosphere felt as thick and heavy as molasses, like the air before a thunderstorm. Except that the storm was taking place inside her. It was suddenly imperative to shift the conversation to more neutral ground. "I won't stand by while you risk Genie's life riding those enormous horses of yours when she's much too young.''

A cloud crossed his features and she knew her strategy had worked, but the satisfaction she expected to feel was absent, replaced by something more like disappointment. "I began riding at the same age. If she's properly taught, there's no danger. Putting her at risk is the last thing I want after all I went through to get her back." He took a deep breath. "Will you believe me when I say she means more to me than my life?"

Something in his tone brought her head up and she was shocked at the depth of pain she found in his expression. He had paled and the character lines around his eyes were more deeply drawn. Her eyes traveled to where his hands gripped the back of a chair. The knuckles were white. She resisted the urge to go to him. "What is it, James? You look ill."

He nodded, wincing as if the movement cost him. "Headache, that's all. I think I will have that drink now. Join me?"

"No, thank you."

She watched as he poured a stiff scotch over ice and downed half of it in a quick toss. An uncomfortable sensation took hold inside her. Was Genie the only problem here? He intercepted her look of concern and misread it completely. "Don't worry, this is a rarity for me. Genevieve won't be living with a drunk."

As he lifted the glass in an ironic toast, it slid from his fingers. He swore as the glass crashed to the floor, shattering on the edge of the bar on the way down.

Thoroughly alarmed now, she went to him. "Something *is* the matter."

His brow furrowed and he flexed his arm and shoulder. "Arm went numb. Probably due to the headache. It's nothing." He bent to gather up the shards of glass.

Although he protested, she helped him. "Has this happened before?"

He slid the fragments into a wastebasket and met her anxious look with a fierce glare. "Your concern is a bit sudden, isn't it? A moment ago you were ready to boil me in oil."

And a moment before that she'd been transported by his kiss and the heady feel of his arms around her, she recalled uncomfortably. Now he was obviously hurting and it tugged at her in a way she didn't care to examine too closely. Telling herself it was simple concern for another human being didn't help. "I believe in fighting fair. You were fully functional then," she snapped at him.

Their heads were close together as they gathered up the broken glass. Without warning, his unaffected arm shot around her waist and he pulled her hard against him as he brought them both upright. "I'm still...fully functional," he said in a warning tone. A frisson of half-alarm, half-anticipation shrilled through her.

Where the moment might have led, she was not to discover because he was interrupted by a brisk knock on the office door. "Is everything all right? I heard glass breaking."

It was Grace McGovern's voice. With a look that clearly promised, "Later for this," James released Zoe and went to the door, opening it to admit the stud manager. Zoe was aware of how her flushed face and slightly disheveled appearance must look, but she held herself straighter, leaving James to explain if he chose. "I dropped a glass. No big deal," he said dismissively.

Grace's sweeping glance took in James's set face. "The arm again?"

He gave a slight shrug. "It's not important. How is Genevieve?"

What was not important? What did Grace mean by

again? James obviously wasn't about to enlighten Zoe, evidently believing that one kiss didn't give her the right to an explanation. He was quite possibly right, but it hurt all the same.

"Genevieve's fine. She's in the house having a glass of milk," Grace assured them, taking her cue from James.

"No aftereffects from her fall?"

It was James who asked, but Grace turned to Zoe to deliver the answer. "None at all. She couldn't wait to get back on. Genevieve has the hands and feet of a born rider."

James shot Zoe an I-told-you-so look, but she refused to be placated. "All the same, I'll check on her myself," she insisted and was halfway back to the house before either of them could object.

Apart from a couple of small bruises, Genie's fall had done her no harm. She begged Zoe to allow her to eat lunch with the stable staff and scampered off without a backward glance the moment Zoe gave reluctant assent. It was a bleak portent, she thought. If the prospect of a solitary lunch held this much anguish, how on earth was she to endure a life without her precious child?

The main dining room with its wonderful soaring timber ceiling was deserted, so Zoe asked for her lunch to be served out on the pergola-covered terrace. She was picking desultorily at a chicken salad when James dropped into a chair opposite her. Apart from a certain strain around his eyes he looked much better. "Dining alone?"

She glanced around. "I don't seem to have much choice. As you pointed out, Genie has practically taken up residence in the stables. How do you feel?"

He rotated his arm at the shoulder experimentally. "Fine, thanks, Grace gave me one of her neck and shoulder massages."

Without thinking, she said, "I could have done it for you if I'd known it would help."

He allowed a long moment to pass. "I got the impression you wanted your hand on my neck—but not to massage it. But I'll bear the offer in mind."

Why hadn't she kept her fool mouth shut? The last thing she wanted to do was touch him, even in the line of duty. She was relieved when the cook interrupted to deposit a plate of fettucine with pesto sauce in front of James. Then he helped himself to iced tea from a pitcher on the table.

"Does Grace know about Genie?" Zoe asked.

He nodded. "The McGoverns managed a property I owned before White Stars. After Ruth left, they stuck by me through all the months of searching for Genevieve. As you've seen, they're already besotted with her."

Feeling like a fifth wheel, Zoe shoved the food around her plate listlessly. Instead of reassuring her that Genie was in good hands, his comment had the opposite effect. It meant Zoe wouldn't even be missed when she returned to Sydney.

He watched her carefully. "You'll still have a place in Genevieve's life if you want it," he offered. "You're important to her."

But not important to him. He hadn't bothered to deny that winning Zoe over was merely a means to an end. "I'm glad you acknowledge that much," she said stiffly.

His eyebrows flickered. "I've never denied it. We both have adjustments to make."

Before Zoe could point out that she was doing most of the adjusting, Genie bounded up to the table. Automatically Zoe reached for her napkin and dabbed at a streak of tomato sauce on the child's cheek. A pang shot through her as she wondered how many more times she'd be doing this.

As soon as she could, Genie squirmed free and turned to James. "Is Mummy coming camping with us tomorrow?"

He gave Zoe a level look. "Why don't we ask her now?"

Zoe fought a surge of alarm. "Nobody said anything about camping." She didn't even try to keep the accusation out of her voice.

"I was coming to it," he said, looking caught-out.

Anger suffused her. "First you put her on a horse higher than her head. Now you want to take her Lord-knows-where into the bush. She's four years old, for goodness' sake. What if she gets frightened, or hurt?"

"All the more reason for you to come along," he said pointedly with maddening logic.

Her sense of panic intensified. The idea of spending a night out in the bush with James unnerved her far more than she wanted him to know. "I've never been camping. I wouldn't know what to do," she disclosed. "And surely Genie's too young anyway."

He flashed a glance at the little girl, but she had dropped to her knees and was examining a ladybird with total absorption. "She mustn't ride, she can't go camping. If I hadn't found her in time, she'd spend her life wrapped in cotton wool."

His lowered tone didn't conceal his anger. Well, he wasn't the only one. "Wrapping her in cotton wool isn't the same as trying to keep her safe," she said in a furious undertone. "I won't let you goad me out of keeping that trust."

"Then you'll come with us?"

"Yes, damn you." It was out before she could stop herself.

A slight smile lifted the corners of his mouth. "Good. We set off after breakfast tomorrow."

Chapter Seven

What had she gotten herself into? Zoe wondered the next morning. She must be crazy agreeing to spend a night out in the bush with James, even with Genie as chaperone. Adding insult to injury, the sun was shining out of an impossibly blue sky, spangling the giant blue gums and olive-clad hills with gold. There would be no reprieve due to the weather.

Nor could she pretend to be ill. Knowing James, he would simply take Genie camping by himself, a far more alarming option. Zoe had no choice but to make the best of it. She resolved to spend as little time alone with James as she possibly could.

After breakfast James loaded her things into a four-wheel-drive vehicle, which looked to have traveled many more kilometers through rugged country than the sleek Branxton Turbo he drove in the city. Come to think of it, James himself had a more rawboned look today than when she had first seen him.

A lump filled her throat as she watched the play of muscles beneath his close-fitting denim shirt, which was tucked into moleskin trousers the color of driftwood. He looked the picture of rugged Australian manhood, the effect emphasized by the battered Akubra hat sitting well back on his chestnut hair.

An array of equipment and sleeping bags was already on board. Zoe inspected the gear in confusion. "I don't see a tent anywhere."

He looked pleased. "The term 'camping' isn't exactly accurate when it comes to Blue Gum Camp. It's a permanent cabin complete with wooden flooring, mosquito nets...and running water," he added, obviously enjoying her openmouthed reaction.

"You let me think you wanted Genie to sleep under canvas in the middle of the bush somewhere," she snapped. What an idiot she had made of herself.

"Only because you're determined to cast me as a heartless brute when it comes to her. If you'd let me explain instead of flying off the handle yesterday, I'd have reassured you about the kind of trip I had planned." He paused, one long-fingered hand grasping the vehicle's door handle. "This isn't about toughening her up. I want Genevieve to feel at home at White Stars. Getting out into the bush will let her experience the heart and soul of the place and make her feel part of it."

"The way I felt about this area as a child," Zoe said involuntarily as memories came flooding back. "My grandfather took me canoeing, swimming and bushwalking through the forests not far from here. Poppa's favorite trail started at the end of Bangalow Road and followed the slope down to Gap Creek." She stopped, her voice choking with emotion.

"Then you can hardly deny Genevieve the same experience, can you?"

It wasn't the same, she thought furiously. In taking her

into the bush her grandparents had wanted nothing more than to share with her their favorite places. It would never have occurred to them to try to win her away from her parents, although there were times when she would have given anything to be able to live permanently in this area. Her grandparents had given her a comforting sense of security and belonging she'd never known with her rootless mother and father.

"I'm not denying her anything," she snapped back. "I'm here, aren't I?"

"In body, anyway," he concluded.

"What more do you want?"

His eyebrow lifted and his appreciative gaze roved over her, from her figure-hugging denims all the way to her sun-streaked curls, tied back with a georgette scarf, which matched her blouse. "I doubt if you're asking me what I want personally. I gave you the answer yesterday, Zoe. But I'd be happy to repeat the demonstration if you're still in doubt."

A shiver traveled along her spine. Yesterday, holding her in his arms, he had answered questions she hadn't even known she was asking. Even telling herself his lovemaking was a means to an end failed to reduce the impact on her senses. Today was another matter. "I'll see if Genie's ready to go," she said hastily. His knowing chuckle followed her escape into the house.

In spite of her apprehension the journey was far more pleasant than she had expected. James was an expert off-road driver, handling the rough terrain with such skill that the dirt roads smoothed out before them. The worst parts were a couple of steep hill climbs where the car threatened to lose traction, but he managed to hold their momentum steady. And each time they crested a hill, they were rewarded with fresh vistas of rain forests, sandstone cliffs, waterfalls and eucalypt glades.

Genie was beside herself with excitement whenever she spotted movement beside the track, shrieking with delight when they had to slow to allow a fat wombat to amble across their path. Then James started a chorus of "Row, Row, Row Your Boat" and by the time they came within sight of Blue Gum Camp even Zoe was singing at the top of her voice.

Camp was definitely a misnomer, she decided as James unlocked a charming timber building nestled amid groves of tall, straight gum trees. The cabin was finished in cedar, with locally milled hardwood ceiling beams and a traditional corrugated iron roof. Inside, the walls were paneled with radiata pine and the furniture was hand-carved in rustic style.

Downstairs were two single beds piled with cushions, which doubled as sofas during the daytime, a cast iron potbellied stove providing cooking and warmth, and an old-fashioned washstand with period-style brass fittings.

On the windowpane above one of the beds was scratched in old-fashioned handwriting, March 27, 1864. James saw her reading it. "One of the pioneers of this land, Laura Dunkell, is said to have scratched the date with her diamond engagement ring a week before her wedding to Jamieson Langford. They spent their wedding night in this cabin."

It was disturbingly easy for Zoe to imagine the little timber dwelling as a romantic retreat, probably lit by candles then, their flickering shadows drawing the night in around the lovers like a cloak.

"Of course, there was a big old double bed here in those days," James went on as if reading her thoughts. "Laura and Jamieson supposedly conceived the first of their fourteen children in it that night."

Zoe balked at the images running riot through her thoughts and the intimacy his description conjured up. Was there a purpose behind James bringing her to the wilderness? With a child in tow, there would be little opportunity for seduction, she was forced to admit, but the very idea speared her with excitement. She directed her anger into a critical glare. "I thought you said you bought this land only a couple of years ago."

He nodded. "It was in the Langford family for over a century until my grandfather gambled it away. Buying it back was my goal for as long as I can remember."

"Do you always achieve your goals?" she asked, thinking of his single-minded search for Genie.

"Those that are within a man's power," he said without elaboration. She wondered what might be beyond this remarkable man's power, but life and death were the only ones she could conceive of. The thought produced a shiver of apprehension for some unaccountable reason.

She dismissed it by examining the rest of the cabin. Up a narrow wooden staircase, a loft area contained another bed festooned with a mosquito net hung from the ceiling. Genie scampered up the stairs ahead of Zoe who went halfway then climbed down again.

"Can I sleep up here?" Genie called, peering down at them, her head barely topping the timber balustrade that edged the loft area.

James actually glanced at Zoe in consultation and she nodded. "If you like."

He gave her a lopsided grin. "Historic moment. I think we just agreed on something. This calls for a celebration."

"Why do I suspect you planned for her to sleep up there all along?"

"Because it means you'll be down here with me."

Feeling flustered because she hadn't considered this most obvious consequence, she looked away, pretending rapt interest in the view from the open front door. It would have been less disturbing if James had taken the loft bed, leaving

Genie to share with Zoe downstairs. But it was too late to alter the arrangement now, Genie was already bouncing on the loft bed, having swathed the mosquito netting around herself to create a secret hideaway.

Zoe tried anyway. "What if she's scared during the night? Or walks in her sleep?"

"You're close by, and there's a safety gate at the top of the stairs to keep her from wandering," he said pointedly. "Face it, you're sleeping with me."

"Sleeping in the same room," she said, correcting him as a tingling sensation wound its way from the back of her neck all the way down her body. Sleeping was probably wishful thinking anyway. She was unlikely to get a wink of rest with James occupying the other bed, barely an arm's width away.

He regarded her with undisguised amusement, the sparkle in his eyes reminding her abruptly of Genie when she was up to mischief. Like father like daughter? It was thoroughly disquieting, given the kind of mischief that would probably appeal to James.

She shook herself mentally and turned her attention to more mundane matters. "What do we do about lunch?"

"The cook packed some chicken kebabs. I'll barbecue them while you make some salad. You'll find the ingredients in the Esky."

So much for seduction, she thought irritably, then chided herself. She was annoyed when he turned her on and annoyed when he didn't. Some people were never satisfied.

A search of the cooler turned up a container of ready-prepared salad, so all she had to do was add the dressing she found in a plastic bottle. By the time she carried the bowl outside, the air was blue with smoke from the open fire and fragrant with the succulent smell of barbecuing meat. A kookaburra eyed them hungrily from a nearby branch. When James tossed a chunk of meat into the air, the bird swooped and caught it before it had a chance to hit the ground.

Genie clapped her hands delightedly. "Can I try?"

James gave her some meat and the kookaburra repeated the trick. Zoe couldn't remember ever seeing the little girl so happy. At some level did the child know this was her land? Much as it pained Zoe to admit it, Genie had the blood of the Dunkells and Jamieson Langford in her veins. What ties did she have with Zoe herself which could possibly compare?

The thought cast a shadow over her enjoyment of the meal, although the char-grilled chicken kebabs were delicious. It was followed by twists of damper, the bread dough being wrapped around the end of a stick and cupped at the end with a finger. They roasted the twists in the fire until crisp all around, then James showed them how to spoon golden syrup into the dent at the top. It made a novel dessert, although Genie had to be reminded to let the damper cool a little before she ate it off the stick.

The meal was washed down with drinks kept cool in the Esky—lemon cordial for Genie and a locally produced Hunter Valley Semillon for James and Zoe. Around them the bush drowsed although James assured Genie that the abundant wildlife would emerge around sunset. He explained that during the day the shy kangaroos and wallabies retreated to the deep shade and slept the hours away.

Zoe knew just how they felt. The wooden bench on which she sat allowed her to rest against the sun-warmed timbers of the cabin. The ever-present drone of insects and the chatter of the birds, added to the effect of the food and wine, combined to lull her into a heavy-lidded torpor.

The cabin in the clearing was a perfect setting for a honeymoon, she thought dreamily. All at once, her mind filled with a vision of herself and James, arriving to spend their wedding night here. With an odd certainty, she knew it was their wedding night because of the way he lifted her, laughing, into his arms to carry her across the threshold. And also because of the delicious thrill of anticipation she felt surging through her.

She wasn't alone. In the dark pools of his eyes, she saw such fierce desire for her that it was just as well she was in his arms because her legs wouldn't have been able to support her.

They didn't have to. When he set her on her feet, he kept a strong arm around her, bracing her, as his mouth found hers. Flames leapt through her, searing away the last remaining barriers between them.

His touch ignited a brushfire within her, the flames tearing along every nerve ending until she trembled with the force of her answering desire. She gasped as he slid the straps of her fuchsia silk going-away dress off her shoulders and pressed his lips to the sensitive hollow at the base of her throat then trailed kisses across her breasts. Her nipples hardened and the cabin spun around her.

"How much do you want me?" James asked, his rasping tone a reminder that he, too, had counted the days until they could be alone like this.

There was only one answer. "I want you more than I ever thought it was possible to want a man."

His eyes gleamed a challenge. "In your bed, or in your life?"

Her head lifted and her jaw firmed. "Both, James. Everything I am and everything I have is yours for the taking."

He needed no second invitation. With a groan of capitulation, he slid his hand under her knees and lifted her against his chest again, hugging her tightly before he placed her carefully on the old-fashioned bed that took up one corner of the cabin.

Her breathing became ragged as she watched him strip

off his white linen shirt, revealing a broad expanse of tanned chest. When his hands went to the zipper of his pants, her tension mounted almost beyond bearing. Soon, she promised herself, she would know the ecstasy of his possession and he would know, beyond doubt, how much he was loved in return.

When James stretched out full-length beside her, she thought she would explode with happiness. In wonder, she lifted a hand to his cheek, noting the rasp of a day's growth of beard against her knuckles. He turned his face into her palm, kissing it, and a smile of pure joy spilled across her features.

Gradually, she became aware that the roughness under her hand came, not from a day-old beard, but from the timber boards of the cabin. She had fallen asleep, and her head was resting against the cabin wall.

She sat up, feeling her face flame. The vividness of the daydream left her feeling shaken. Her fantasy must have been fueled by James's talk about his forebears spending their honeymoon night in the cabin. How else could she explain the vision of James carrying her over the cabin threshold and taking her to bed as if it was his right as her husband?

It wasn't as if she wanted it to happen. So what was going on here?

She looked around. The lunch things had been cleared away and the fire doused. The shadows were much deeper. How long had she drowsed?

When she scouted around the immediate area, she found no sign of James or Genie. Despite her inclinations, she knew better than to set off in search of them. This was still untamed wilderness and it was easy to get lost. She suppressed a shiver of apprehension. Had Genie somehow wandered off and James had gone to look for her? Surely he would have alerted Zoe?

Her anger grew and she hugged her arms across her chest. Even if they'd only gone for a walk, they should have let her know instead of allowing her to wake up alone and disoriented, her imagination going into overdrive. If something did happen to them, she wouldn't know where to start looking.

Fear fueled her anger until she was fuming by the time they walked out of the rain forest into the clearing. Relief swept through her as Genie ran up to her, her smile wide and her eyes alight. "Guess what we found, Mummy?"

Zoe turned blazing eyes on James but managed to keep her anger in check as she hugged the child. The feel of Genie's small, warm body next to her heart dragged at her like a physical pain and she blinked hard to clear her brimming eyes. "What did you find, sweetheart?"

"Animal tracks. James showed me what made them. Look." Squirming out of Zoe's embrace, Genie dropped to the ground. "This is a koala, and this is a kangaroo."

With her finger in the dust the little girl drew a mark like a child's handprint for the koala and a track in the shape of a V with the inside arm almost twice the length of the outside arm for the kangaroo. "And if you want to see a koala, you have to look down, not up," Genie continued, almost breathless with excitement. "James showed me the funny-shaped poo they leave under their tree so you know there's a koala up in the branches."

"James is a regular fountain of knowledge," Zoe commented dryly, the irony in her tone directed unmistakably at the man in question. He might be Genie's father, but he had no right to take her off into the bush where anything might have happened to her. Zoe managed to restrain her temper long enough to send Genie inside to wash her hands and rest on her bed with a picture book until dinnertime.

Left alone with James, Zoe couldn't help remembering the man in her daydream and the way the bush air had been charged with the force of the love between them. When he had carried her into the cabin, his desire for her had been unmistakable, as he embraced her tightly enough to threaten her breathing.

It was only a fantasy, she reminded herself. She mustn't confuse a daydream with fact. James would never be her lover, far less her husband and the father of her children. The only child he wanted was Genie. His behavior this afternoon clearly demonstrated it.

"Did you have a pleasant rest?" he asked.

She tossed her head. "No thanks to you. How do you think I felt waking up to find you and Genie missing?"

He frowned. "Hardly missing. You looked so peaceful it seemed a shame to wake you up."

She felt anything but peaceful now. His nearness reminded her forcefully of her dream—of what she could never have. The yearning pulled at her, making her achingly conscious of him. Braced with his legs apart and palms grazing his hips, he looked as tall and immutable as the giant blue gums around them. She dragged in a deep breath. "All the same, you could have told me you were taking her." Angry with herself for the betraying tremor coloring her voice, she brushed her forehead with the back of her hand. "If anything had happened—" She broke off, horrified at how close she had come to saying, "to you."

The fight ebbed out of him. "You're entitled to be upset. I should have told you before we left. Of all people, I know how it feels to have your loved ones vanish without explanation."

The abrupt change swept her defenses aside. "It's all right," she heard herself saying. "You don't need my permission to go for a walk."

His gaze hardened again as his expression underwent a sea change. "I wasn't suggesting I did. While I regret causing you undue concern, you need to understand that Genevieve is my daughter. She's now in my care, and I will decide what's best for her.''

A shiver shook Zoe, not only because the sun was low in the sky. At his blunt reminder of her status, iced water trickled along her veins. "Don't feel you have to spare my feelings," she said sarcastically. "Ruth warned me what you were really like."

Anger clouded his features, but his voice was rigidly controlled as he demanded, "This sounds fascinating. Based on Ruth's testimony, unreliable though it was, what have you decided I'm *really* like?"

She had nothing left to lose. "You're a heartless tyrant who only cares about getting your own way. You don't want a child. You want living proof of your virility."

As soon as the words were out of her mouth Zoe wished she could snatch them back. She had allowed worry over Genie's absence to overcome reason. Her brief taste of his virility made the accusation not only stupid but reckless in the extreme. "I shouldn't have said that," she murmured, unnerved by the fierceness inflaming his expression.

"You think I need to prove my virility?" he asked in a dangerous, low voice.

The devil's choice loomed before her. If she said no, she admitted that he had already proved it to her. If she said yes, she invited a demonstration. She lifted her head, meeting his gaze with a certainty she was far from feeling. "Do you?"

For answer he dropped his hands to her shoulders and pulled her against him until her breasts were crushed against his chest. Through her filmy blouse, the heat of his fingers seeped along her bones, pooling deep in her core until she arched against him in unthinking response.

With a muffled gasp, he tightened his hold and his mouth closed over hers, warm, sensual, giving and demanding all at once. Her senses reeled. This wasn't a kiss. This was a gift, a threat, a promise, although of what, she hardly dared consider. She only knew that no man had ever affected her like this.

She wasn't alone, she realized distantly. James's breathing came in sharp gasps and tremors swept through him in time with the unmistakable pulsing of his need. She had done that to him, driving him close to the limits of control, she thought on a surge of elation. She might only be a hindrance to him, but he wouldn't forget her in a hurry.

It came to her that she wouldn't easily forget him. For a long time, every man would be measured against James's overwhelming masculinity. Every kiss would be compared with the fire he ignited in her blood.

Try as she might she couldn't make herself regret the fact. If he did no more than kiss her like this, James had given her a taste of what a real man might offer her, and what she could give in return. Married to Andrew, with no other basis for comparison, she might have gone to her grave in ignorance.

James stepped away from her, anger vibrating in every line of his stance. "Do you still think Ruth told you the truth about me?"

Pride wouldn't let her reveal the full extent of his impact on her. "She didn't describe what you were like as a lover, so I wouldn't know," she raged at him. "But if you were as high-handed with her as you are with me, it's no wonder she couldn't wait to get away."

He looked as if he would like to break something in two, his powerful hands flexing at his sides. He siphoned off the energy by pacing to the edge of the clearing, pausing to speak over his shoulder. "For your information, I wasn't the reason Ruth left. The truth is, she was jealous of Genevieve."

"Jealous? I don't understand."

"She didn't want to share me with anyone, not even her

own child. No matter how much I assured her of my love, she resented any attention I gave to the baby, however minimal. She saw Genevieve as her rival and couldn't stand it.''

Unwillingly Zoe recalled how Ruth had brushed aside reports of her baby's progress yet eagerly regaled Zoe with details of her own activities when she came to collect Genie at the end of each day. Nevertheless, there were two sides to every story. ''Perhaps she found it hard to cope alone after you returned to the Middle East,'' she ventured.

His eyes darkened. ''She was hardly alone. She had Grace and her husband as well as a full staff dancing attendance on her.''

But she didn't have the most vital support—her husband's. Zoe avoided voicing the thought. She was only too well aware of how lonely it felt to lack the support of the most important person in your life.

James read her expression anyway. ''Just because I was kept apart from my family doesn't mean I didn't care. They were in my thoughts every minute of every day I was away. Not all men are like your late husband, Zoe.''

The blunt reminder that his investigation had included an assessment of Andrew's character made Zoe recoil in shock, but she forced herself to focus on the present. ''Then why didn't you come back?''

He ran wiry fingers through the thick waves of his hair. ''Do you think I haven't blamed myself for that ever since Ruth took Genevieve away? I can't change what happened. But I can move heaven and earth to ensure nothing comes between us ever again.''

Nothing and no one, including her, Zoe read between the lines. Once again there was no attempt to explain his delayed return and, if truth be told, it had nothing to do with her. Finding out he was caught up with business or had a mistress in the Middle East might make it easier to blame him, but it wouldn't change the present situation. Even the impact of their kiss wouldn't alter his course, although she was sure he had felt it as strongly as she had. He intended to take Genie back, end of discussion.

She was beginning to accept that her child was lost to her, she realized. She wouldn't put it past James to have arranged this trip to wear down her resistance. Despite her previous suspicions, seduction hadn't been part of his plan. His kiss was too spontaneous and far, far too mutual, she'd swear to it. But he could show what a splendid father he was. She had already begun to accept him in that role—and herself as beaten.

To hell with that, she thought fiercely. Maybe she was beaten. But not yet. James was staring out into the bush, his back turned to her. His broad shoulders were set and he gripped the low branch of a eucalypt as if he would snap it.

She strode across the clearing and reached to touch his shoulder. When he turned around she gasped in shock. Underneath his tan his skin looked gray. His mouth was compressed into a tight line and perspiration beaded his forehead. His eyes were cloudy with suffering.

"James, what is it?" she asked. When he didn't seem to hear, she touched the back of her hand to his forehead and he winced as if the light touch hurt. "My God, you're on fire."

"Headache," he rasped. "Hit me out of the blue."

"Can I get you something, some medication?"

Speaking seemed to cost him an effort. "Didn't bring anything with me."

She remembered the first-aid kit in her bag. "I have some painkillers with me. They're not very strong, but they might help a little. I'll get them. For goodness' sake sit down. You look as if you're about to fall down."

His lack of argument spoke volumes as he pried himself

free of the branch and allowed her to guide him to the picnic setting where he settled as if felled. She was back in seconds with the painkillers and he gulped them down, beyond noticing that she sat with him until they took effect.

When he had recovered sufficiently, she stood up. "These headaches can't be normal. I'm taking you back to the homestead so you can see a doctor tonight."

"You and whose army?" he asked, cocking an eyebrow at her.

He was definitely improving. "I don't need an army. I own the painkillers." It was cruel, but all was fair with a patient as stubborn as James.

He grinned shakily. "You know how to hurt a man when he's down."

She affected a shrug, more worried than she wanted him to know. "Whatever works."

He climbed to his feet, the effort not lost on her. "It isn't fair to you and Genevieve to have me collapse in the middle of the bush, so I'll come quietly, officer."

She snorted. "That'll be the day."

He sobered. "I won't be much good behind the wheel. Can you handle a four-wheel-drive?"

She hadn't thought of that, but she couldn't back out now. James needed medical help, and he wouldn't get it in the wilderness. She squared her shoulders. "Now is as good a time as any for me to learn."

Chapter Eight

Thanks to Zoe's painkillers, the throbbing headache gradually dulled to a tolerable ache, but James knew the relief wouldn't last. He cursed himself for not packing his medication, but he'd been sure he could manage without it for one night and it didn't go with driving in any case.

Fat lot of good that bit of bravado had done him. Now he didn't have either the painkillers or the steadiness of vision to tackle the bush track in the dark. He wasn't fooled by Zoe's assurance that she could handle it. Wilderness driving was a challenge for an experienced driver. To someone new to off-road vehicles it was unthinkable.

She made a habit of doing the unthinkable, he noticed with a surge of unwilling admiration. Dragging herself out of the mire of a bad marriage to remake her life and career after her husband died. Making a home for Genevieve when her family couldn't be traced. Coming with him to White Stars when it was probably the last place Zoe wanted to be.

He had to hand it to her. She was a fighter.

She was incredibly passionate, too, judging from the all-too-brief kiss they had shared. His investigators had reported that her late husband had been jealously possessive, so she probably didn't know the half of it herself. Exploring her full potential in that area would be a positive pleasure—for both of them, James thought, then chided himself. It was pointless to torment himself with the remembered warmth of her mouth or the softness of her slender body in his arms when he could offer her only an uncertain future. Today's fiasco proved it beyond doubt.

He made himself get up and move. Luckily they hadn't fully unloaded the car so it wouldn't take long to get under way. Zoe had already gathered up the food and kitchen utensils and had stowed them aboard.

He smiled as Genevieve appeared at the cabin door, dragging a packed sleeping bag in one hand and clutching a Vegemite sandwich in the other. Zoe had managed to make a game of their need to drive home in the dark, turning a potential disappointment into a new adventure. She had short-circuited Genevieve's protests by telling her a story about the possums, wombats and kangaroos and how they were most active at night. Now the little girl couldn't wait to get going.

Funny, but he couldn't recall Ruth ever being so considerate with their child. The sight brought a pang that was hard to dismiss. Zoe was a much better mother than Ruth had ever been. A much better wife? He shoved the thought aside. As the one coming between her and Genevieve, he'd be the last person to interest Zoe. Under the circumstances it was probably just as well.

She looked pale but resolute as she got behind the wheel, and at her shaky smile his respect for her notched even higher. "Ready to go?" she asked.

"Maybe I should drive."

She frowned in denial. "You can barely see straight. And

you daren't take too many more painkillers until you've seen a doctor.''

The hell of it was, she was right. "Very well, let's get under way. Just take it slowly and for Pete's sake watch out for kangaroos bounding across the track in front of us.''

She gave him a what-do-I-look-like glance and slid the powerful vehicle into gear. Like most four-wheel-drives, this one had freewheeling hubs, which James had locked into place for driving off-road. The low-range gears allowed tremendous pressure to be exerted through the tires so the vehicle would grip no matter how muddy, slippery and uneven the terrain. But four-wheel-drives could also get into trouble. They could get bogged and could also roll on steep slopes if not approached head-on.

Zoe handled the first few kilometers easily enough, but the track was reasonably level. While they saw plenty of kangaroos and even one big red who kept pace with them for a distance, none had crossed their path.

She looked at him. "You can breathe out now. I can *do* this.''

"So far,'' he muttered then could have kicked himself. The last thing she needed was him undermining her confidence. He compensated by adding, "You're doing great.''

"How about you? How are you doing?''

"Vision's still blurry but the headache has eased. I'll be fine.'' If she believed that, he thought, then he had a bridge he could sell her. All the same he was relieved when she accepted his assurance at face value and returned her attention to the driving.

In the back seat Genevieve was fast asleep. He felt a momentary pang of envy. What with the painkillers and the stress, he'd give a lot to be able to follow his daughter's example, but the worst hills were ahead of them. Zoe was going to need his guidance to get over them in one piece.

"I enjoyed the story you told Genevieve while we were

packing," he said, hoping conversation would help him to keep alert. "Did you make it up?"

She nodded. "When I was little, I always wanted to be a children's writer."

"You're good at it. What happened?"

In the dim light he saw her shrug. "Life. The need to earn a living. Becoming a nanny let me have a career, somewhere to live and still be able to work with children."

He remembered the details supplied by the private investigator. "Your parents' work took them all over the world, so you couldn't live at home, could you?"

"Why are we even having this discussion?" she muttered furiously. "Your spies have told you everything about me—even, it seems, about my disastrous marriage."

"I only know the bare facts," he asserted. "They don't explain why you made the choices you did or how you felt about them."

"I was young, foolish, and mistook Andrew's fixation on me for love. It wasn't hard because I was already vulnerable. I'd never known a real home, and when you're a nanny, you're always losing the children as they go to school or move away."

No wonder she was finding it so hard to let Genevieve go, he concluded. Finally having a child she thought of as her own must have seemed like a miracle after all the upheavals she'd endured in her life, first with her gypsy-parents and then as a nanny. It was a damned shame. She deserved a lot better. And it didn't improve his mood to know he was adding to her distress.

"Then you can see why it's vital to let me give Genevieve a stable home environment," he stated. "You were hurt by your upbringing. I'm sure you want something better for her."

"My upbringing has nothing to do with this," she

snapped. "I do want what's best for her and I was doing a good job of providing it."

He knew the pain was clouding his judgment, but it didn't help that she refused to listen to reason. "By farming her out to your neighbor or a playgroup whenever your work demanded your attention?" he asked.

She swung the wheel to dodge a tree branch jutting out into the road. "What about *your* work? It was important enough to keep you away from home when Genie was a baby."

He winced and not only because the car's sudden movement jolted his head back against the headrest, making him see stars. When they subsided he said, "Despite what you evidently believe, my work is not my whole life. My greatest satisfaction came from building the business from scratch. Now I'm content to hand over the day-to-day running of the corporation to Brian Dengate. You have to be like a parent whose child has grown, knowing when your job is done and it's time to let go and move on."

Was he sending her a message—let go and move on? Zoe noted that James's advice didn't include any thoughts on how to accomplish this miracle when the child was flesh-and-blood instead of a corporation. Zoe still didn't know how she was going to leave Genie at White Stars when the time came. It would be like leaving a piece of herself behind.

She drove the thought away by concentrating on getting them down the steep hill ahead. Getting up was bad enough, but she could already feel the wheels slipping on the rough surface as they began their descent.

"Easy on the brakes. You don't want to lock up the wheels," James said quietly. "Remember your own words—you can do this."

At his quiet assurance she felt her confidence lift. Easing her foot off the clutch, she slid the car into low-second gear.

This time the back wheels held traction and they made it to the foot of the steep hill without any more problems.

With a good helping of grit and determination and James's quiet encouragement when the going got rough, she managed the rest of the journey without jolting them around too much. Relief washed through her as the lights of the homestead came into view. She had never seen a more welcome sight in her life.

"The car phone might work now that we're out of the shadow of the ranges," James suggested. "I'll let Grace know we're coming home early but that everything's all right."

It wasn't all right, but she let it pass and he contacted the homestead on the speaker phone. Over James's protests she insisted he have Grace contact James's local doctor who lived on a neighboring property. With luck he would be at home and not at his surgery in Cooranbong, a good forty minutes' drive away.

It was the first lucky break of the day. The doctor, Howard Leigh, was not only at home, Grace reported when they arrived at the homestead, but he was indulging his hobby of astronomy, using a powerful telescope set up in a paddock close to the boundary of White Stars. His wife had been able to contact him by mobile phone.

Zoe gave a sigh of relief. "Then Dr. Leigh can get here soon?"

Grace nodded and James moved restlessly. "It's a waste of his time when there's nothing he can do."

"We'll see," Zoe said equably but fear wrapped a relentless fist around her heart and squeezed tightly. She felt faint. James might be the enemy as far as she was concerned, but he was also Genie's father. If anything happened to him...

The realization that her concern wasn't entirely because of Genie sent a rush of heat along her veins. The warmth moved up her body to her face and she was glad that James had left her alone while he got ready for the doctor's visit. Today, when he took her in his arms in the wilderness, the strength of her reaction had alarmed her. With very little encouragement he would have become her lover.

Yet no matter how dizzyingly enticing she found the idea—and she could no longer deny it to herself, she *did* find him more enticing than any man she had ever met— he had no interest in her beyond her involvement with Genie. And he had already shown his determination to sever that particular tie. Letting herself get involved with him would be downright crazy.

All the same she found it uncommonly hard to focus on anything while the doctor was with James. True to his word Howard Leigh had arrived promptly. Although without the traditional medical bag, he would have been hard to identify as a doctor. He wore baggy jeans and a sloppy, grass-stained sweater and his hair stood up in spikes.

When he saw Zoe standing in the doorway, he regarded her with interest. "I was expecting Grace to let me in. She didn't warn me that James was...entertaining," he observed with a slight wink.

"He isn't...entertaining." She echoed the doctor's tone, pregnant pause and all. Let him wonder about her relationship to the family.

The doctor grinned. "Pity, he should be. I'll be sure to tell him so."

Before she could respond the doctor strode along the hall toward James's room, evidently well familiar with the layout of the house. It was left to Zoe to wonder what rumors had been spreading around the district about her presence at White Stars, as well as why she should care what anyone thought.

Or why the doctor's choice of words should resonate in her mind. *Pity.*

She was on her third cup of coffee, halfheartedly picking at a sandwich in lieu of the dinner they had managed to miss, when the doctor emerged. He refused her offer of coffee. "No, thanks. I'm on comet-watch tonight. Got to get back to it."

"It was good of you to interrupt your free evening," she said automatically. "How is James?"

Dr. Leigh frowned. "Not good, but then it's hardly surprising. You did the right thing getting him back here and calling me."

"What is it? What's the matter with him?"

The doctor appeared to weigh his options. "You seem to care a great deal about James for someone he isn't *entertaining*," he said after a long pause. "But I can't break patient confidentiality. If James wants you to know what's wrong with him, he'll have to tell you himself. I've given him something for the headache so he should get a good night's rest."

What about *her* night's rest, she wanted to ask. She was more worried about what the doctor hadn't said, than what he had. But he would reveal no more and finally left to resume his stargazing.

Grace had already returned to her own house and Genie was fast asleep in her own bed, having hardly stirred when Zoe carried her from the car to her room. So there was nothing for Zoe to do except tidy the kitchen, shower and go to bed herself and hope she could manage a few hours' sleep.

She awoke with a start and lay, heart pounding, wondering what had disturbed her. The house was silent and she didn't need to look at her watch to see that the first fingers of dawn were barely streaking across the sky. She sat upright and swung her legs over the side of the bed, reaching for her dressing gown. Had Genie called out, the sound penetrating Zoe's exhausted sleep?

It seemed not. When Zoe looked in, she found the child asleep on her back, her chestnut curls spilling across the pillow. One arm was flung over her head and the other tightly clutched Big Ted.

Zoe tiptoed in and pulled the covers up to Genie's chest, her mouth softening into a smile. "I love you," she whispered, kissing her finger and touching it lightly to the child's forehead. When she didn't stir, Zoe tiptoed out again, closing the door behind her, her heart swelling with anguish. How was she going to endure a life without such moments? It was almost more than she could bear to contemplate.

She debated returning to bed but knew she was unlikely to go back to sleep, so she settled for going to the kitchen to make herself a hot drink. People stirred early in the country, so she wouldn't be the only one awake for long.

She wasn't the only one awake now, she saw when she took her drink outside to the terrace. A light shone in what she identified as James's office above the stables complex. Dr. Leigh had prescribed rest. He wouldn't be pleased to find his patient up and working at this hour of the morning.

Unless he was still in pain and hadn't wanted to disturb anyone else, she thought fearfully. James must have been the one who awakened her when he went outside, she thought, pausing to wonder when she had become so sensitive to his movements.

Before she had the thought fully hatched, she set her cup down and walked across to the stables, which were deeply shadowed and quiet. Only the soft whickering of the horses as she passed their stalls marked her presence. Either James didn't hear, or he assumed it was one of the staff because he didn't come down to investigate.

She found him staring out the window at the ribbons of red and gold streaking the dawn sky. He turned slightly when she pushed the door open. "Mind if I come in?"

"Feel free. There's coffee in the percolator if you'd like some." He didn't sound surprised to see her.

Her first cup was still on the terrace, so she poured coffee for herself and carried it to where he stood at the window. "Couldn't sleep? Me, neither."

He gave a dismissive shrug. "I needed to do some thinking while everything's quiet. I didn't wake you, did I?"

In all honesty she didn't know, so she shook her head. "Aren't you supposed to be resting?"

He gave a harsh laugh, which held little in the way of humor. "Not you, too. I got enough of a lecture from Howard Leigh last night about the folly of going off to Blue Gum Camp."

She took a sip of coffee as tension spiraled through her and settled in a tight knot in her stomach. "Why did you go if you aren't well?"

"Because I thought it might be for the last time."

His matter-of-fact statement cut to the core of her fears. Something must be seriously wrong to make him think this way. "Something is wrong with you. What is it, James?"

He turned a disturbingly direct look on her. "Howard Leigh didn't tell you?"

"He said I should ask you. So I'm asking." She took a deep breath. "I realize it's none of my business, but you are Genie's father." And I do care about you, she added but kept this last to herself. She had a feeling he wouldn't want to hear it.

She was right. "Feeling sorry for me, Zoe?" His tone was coldly ironic as if it was the last thing he expected from her.

"How can I until you tell me what's wrong?" she asked, apprehension gripping her so tightly it was hard to breathe suddenly.

He dragged in a deep breath and turned to face her.

"Very well. I have a bullet in me that stands a good chance of killing me."

The room started to spin around her and she reached for the nearest support, which happened to be James himself. His arm circled her automatically, his strength buoying her up until she regained her balance enough to step away from him even though instinct urged her closer. She felt as if his announcement had scythed the foundations from under her. "A bullet? But how? Why?"

The tension lines in his face relaxed into a ghost of a smile. "Worried about me? This is a first."

She clenched her hands around the coffee cup. "What do you expect when you come out with such an outrageous statement. If this is your idea of a joke..."

The slight smile vanished. "It's no joke. Lord knows, I wish it was. Almost two years ago when I was working in the Middle East I got in the way of a terrorist who objected to foreigners working in his country, no matter how important the contribution being made."

She knew her face was as white as her coffee cup. "He shot you?"

James nodded tautly. "The bullet lodged in my neck near the spine. After the initial wound healed, I had no pain or other symptoms so the doctors decided the bullet was best left where it was, considering surgery to be more risky."

"And now?"

"A few weeks ago the bullet moved. Now the medicos tell me it's pressing against a vital nerve in my spine, causing numbness and tingling in my arm and these blinding headaches, which I'm told will only get worse."

A sense of helplessness overtook her. So much for her suspicion that business or a mistress had kept him away from his family. The truth was far worse than anything she had suspected. Her heart went out to him, but she also sensed that pity was the last thing he would want. "There must be something the doctors can do."

He nodded. "Bill Margolin is an old friend who also happens to be a Macquarie Street specialist. He can't wait to get me onto the operating table."

"What's stopping you?" Fearful though the prospect of surgery might be, she couldn't imagine a man like James letting fear stand in his way. "It's Genie, isn't it?"

His hands balled into fists until he relaxed them with a visible effort. "After Bill told me what was ahead of me, I had the investigators step up their efforts to find her, so if the worst happened I would at least see her secure as my heir. I was all set to schedule the surgery when the investigators told me they'd located her. Then when I met her again, she was so damned sweet I wanted to spend every minute I could with her."

How he must have hated Zoe for accusing him of coming between her and Genie, she thought on a wave of remorse. In his shoes she probably would have behaved exactly the same. Anger at the unfairness of the situation rose in her, as well as a shattering sense of loss, some of which was on her own account, she was forced to recognize. Having tasted the power of his arms and the sweetness of his kiss, she didn't want to think about a world without James Langford in it. Even if they had no future together, he should have a future apart from her. She felt her eyes begin to blur.

He saw her reaction and brushed her lashes with the back of one finger. "Tears, Zoe? I'm not dead yet, you know."

"It would take a lot more than a terrorist's bullet," she retorted, taking refuge in annoyance. Her tears were at the thought of Genie gaining a father only to risk losing him again, that was all. If she told herself often enough, she might even start believing it.

He seemed satisfied. "I used to think so, too, until it

happened. But Bill tells me the surgery has only two possible outcomes—I'll make it or I won't. He was kind enough not to quote me the odds, but I gather they aren't in my favor.''

"What are you going to do?" She tried to match his matter-of-fact approach and knew she failed miserably.

He stilled, weighing the question. She got the impression he'd been weighing it for some time. Then he seemed to reach a decision. "In a way it depends on you."

Surprise brought her head up as fresh apprehension quivered through her. "What do you want me to do?"

"I want you to marry me."

It was the last thing she had expected and shock bubbled through her, turning her legs to jelly. This time she stayed upright under her own power, determined not to let him see that he had stunned her to her core. "You're proposing marriage now, of all times?"

"Especially now. As my wife you would inherit everything I have. With you to care for her and my fortune to provide for you both, Genevieve's future would be secure, no matter what happens on the operating table."

It was a breathtaking notion in more ways than one. Hearing herself described as his wife almost made her miss the last part of his proposal. As the full import caught up with her she drew a strangled breath. "That would be some prenuptial agreement—a marriage certificate and a will all in one."

"Quite possibly."

It was almost beyond her to deal with his proposal on any level. What he suggested wasn't marriage as she understood it. Marriage involved love and caring, intimacy he had no intentions of offering. It was a measure of his desperation that he was offering marriage at all. She was well aware that it was for Genie's sake, not her own.

She struggled to speak around the lump clogging her

throat. "There must be another way to solve this without creating a...a...widow in advance?"

His mouth twisted into a wry imitation of a smile. "I may surprise you and survive the operation."

The lump increased in size but she refused to swallow. "What happens then?"

"Since the marriage would be purely for Genevieve's protection, it will end once it's no longer necessary. You'll have an agreement to that effect before I go into surgery. One month after the operation, if I survive, the marriage will be annulled, although I won't object if you want to keep in touch with Genevieve. You'll have your freedom and enough money from me to ensure you won't want for anything ever again."

How could he think she would accept money from him, especially under such circumstances? It hadn't escaped her that for an annulment to be possible, the marriage would have to be in name only. Given how they felt about each other it was the only sensible course, yet the violent denial that exploded through her caught her unawares and her heart raced in erratic counterpoint.

"Can't you leave everything to Genie without marrying me?" she managed to ask.

His eyes shone derisively. "She's too young to be the target of every fortune hunter in my immediate family. I want her guardianship to be beyond any doubt."

Dimly she remembered her friend, Julie, mentioning that he was estranged from his family. "Yet you're willing to entrust me with everything," she said pointedly, finding the thought of how much he was willing to trust her curiously exhilarating.

His gaze locked with hers. "Since you came to White Stars, I've seen how much my daughter means to you. Unlike the rest of my family, you would put her welfare ahead of your own."

It was precisely what he was asking of her, she thought. Marrying him was a step she had never contemplated, wasn't sure she could contemplate now. It was one thing to marry a man you loved beyond all others. Quite another to agree to a marriage whose end was written before the vows themselves.

More disturbing still was the danger to her peace of mind. James affected her more than any man she had ever known, stoking fires deep within her, which he clearly had no interest in quenching. Could she consider becoming his wife knowing there was no future for them, whatever the outcome of the operation? It was hard enough to contemplate that she might be his widow before she ever was his wife. If he lived—and despite everything, she wished it with all her heart—she would also have outlived her usefulness.

Indecision tore at her. Tears she had refused to shed for herself clustered behind her eyes, for him. There was really only one consideration that mattered—he was Genie's father, facing the worst crisis anyone could have to face. For Genie's sake she knew what her answer must be. "Yes, I'll marry you, James."

His hand shot out and a crooked finger caught a single tear as it slid down her cheek. "I hope these are not for me, Zoe. They would only complicate things."

Stopped in her tracks, she frowned. "What do you mean?"

"You mustn't make the mistake of caring about me. Only the thought that you're doing this for Genevieve will make it work." He smiled tiredly, the humor failing to reach his eyes. "You may think me heartless, but I'm not so unfeeling as to want to leave behind a grieving widow."

"Then it's as well we both know where we stand," she said flatly. It made a bizarre kind of sense as long as she avoided examining her own feelings too closely. "How soon do you want the wedding to take place?"

"As soon as it can be arranged. Both Bill Margolin and Howard Leigh have made it clear I can't put the operation off much longer. If we hold the ceremony on Friday afternoon and have a weekend honeymoon, I can check into the hospital next week."

Less than a week away? She suppressed the panic, which raced through her at the prospect. "Very well."

He lifted a quizzical eyebrow at her. "So composed, Zoe. No other reaction beyond 'very well'?"

The reaction she was tempted to share with him would have brought the house down, she thought, aware that any emotional display would undermine his belief that she was the right person for the task. "I thought not caring was a job qualification." She managed to keep the shakiness out of her voice by a superhuman effort.

His eyes narrowed. "Indeed. I realize I'm asking a lot, Zoe. There are no words for how much I appreciate the sacrifice you'll be making for Genevieve."

But not for himself, she noticed bleakly, even now feeling the impact of the man on every sense she possessed. It set up a throbbing resonance deep inside her, a chorus of needs and demands she would have to subdue before she joined him at the altar, if she was to have any hope of surviving emotionally undamaged.

He came closer. "No regrets? No second thoughts?"

All of those and more, she thought, her mind in turmoil. Somehow she managed to meet his eyes unflinchingly. "Have you?"

"Plenty," he growled as his searching gaze roved over her. He was so alive, so powerful that it was hard to believe he could be facing death on anything but his own terms. "For a long time after Ruth disappeared, I told myself I would never marry again."

If things were different, his vow would stand, she was sure. "I felt the same after Andrew died," she admitted. Unlike James, her certainty had begun to erode, possibly from the moment she met him, although she wasn't about to admit it.

"There's been no man who could change your mind since then?"

"Actually there has," she said, gaining a tiny measure of satisfaction from the tightening of the small lines around his mouth. He might be marrying her under duress, but he wasn't entirely indifferent to her, either. She was woman enough to feel her spirits lift. "I believe he just did."

Chapter Nine

Finding yourself aboard a runaway train must feel like this, Zoe decided. She knew why James couldn't afford any delay, but the prospect of becoming his wife in a matter of days filled her with apprehension.

Telling herself it was for Genie's sake didn't help. No matter how brief the marriage, Zoe would be bound to James in the most intimate of unions and their lives would be linked forever afterward. In the eyes of the world she would be his wife. His ex-wife, if he survived the operation.

His widow, if something went wrong. She choked off the possibility as tension seized her. No matter what the consequences to her, she refused to contemplate such an outcome. James would live. He was a survivor.

"I've made provisions for the wedding to take place at two o'clock on Friday," James said, startling her out of her reverie. She hadn't heard him come out to the terrace where she watched from a discreet distance as Grace gave Genie another riding lesson.

She kept her tone light to quell the nervousness that

threatened to swamp all rational thought. "Is it enough time to make the necessary arrangements?"

"It's all the time we have."

All the time *he* had, she amended silently, the reminder slamming into her with numbing force. How could she agonize over her own problems when James's very life hung in the balance? She lifted her chin. If he could face this with such courage, she would do her part with equal grace. "I'll be ready."

He nodded, his eyes gleaming as if she had surprised him. "Good. I've started the formalities already. A local magistrate and longtime family friend has agreed to perform the ceremony. Is there anyone you want me to invite?"

"Only my friend Julie and her son, Simon, my neighbors from Sydney," she said. Asking other friends or her coworkers from the property consultancy would involve her in too many explanations she didn't feel up to giving.

"What about your mother? She lives in Wollongong, doesn't she?"

Of course, his investigators would have told him about Zoe's mother, too. Instead of rankling, the reminder felt like a relief, although Zoe wondered when she had stopped minding that James knew so much about her. "My mother and I haven't spoken in years, since the time I tried to tell her about my problems with Andrew. She told me I'd made my bed and would have to lie on it."

James set his teeth as if he had his own opinion of such behavior, but all he said was, "Charming."

She recalled the disparaging way he'd spoken about his own family. "What about your relatives?"

"My only sister, Patrice, lives in New Mexico. My father died of a heart condition many years ago. When my mother remarried, she acquired a menagerie of steprelatives whose main interest is in my money. Unfortunately they have no interest in earning any of their own.''

If his steprelatives were a group of fortune hunters, it was no wonder James was so anxious to protect Genie's inheritance. The grim reminder of the reason for this discussion sent a shudder through Zoe.

James's penetrating look swept over her. ''What is it?''

Since his proposal left no room for regrets on her own account, she grasped at another concern, one of the oldest known to womankind. ''I don't have anything suitable to wear. I'll need to borrow the car and go shopping in town. Grace can probably tell me the best place to buy clothes.''

''The local stores are fine for most things, but I hardly think they can conjure up a wedding dress in under a week,'' he observed.

She gave a deep sigh, barely conscious of how much longing she put into the soft sound. ''I don't suppose it matters for our purposes.''

''It matters to me. Come.''

Puzzled, she followed him to a study off the living room where he motioned her to a chair while he punched up a number on the phone. After a short discussion he handed the phone to her. ''Aloys Gada wants to talk to you.''

Her jaw dropped. ''The *designer*, Aloys Gada?''

''In the flesh, or the voice,'' came the amused comment down the line. ''My friend James tells me you need a wedding dress in a hurry.''

''But I can't afford—''

''He says it's his wedding present to you,'' Gada short-circuited her objections. ''I believe I'm to dress a little girl as well.''

The reason for James's generosity became clear. He wanted Genie to have the best of everything, including a stepmother whose appearance wouldn't provoke awkward questions. She decided to cooperate for Genie's sake, but it was hard to suppress a wave of excitement. Andrew hadn't cared for what he called "the trappings" so she had worn a simple cream suit for their registry-office wedding, followed by dinner at a restaurant. As a result, she had never really felt like a bride. It was ironic that this time she would look the part, when everything else would be a sham.

As they discussed dress styles and fabrics, Gada's enthusiasm took wing. When Zoe gave him Genie's measurements then her own, the designer chuckled appreciatively. "No wonder James can't wait to marry you. With those proportions, you're a dream to dress, my dear."

"But how will you—"

"James is sending a helicopter for me tomorrow afternoon. I'll bring a selection of gowns adjusted to fit so you can make your choice."

Gada was as good as his word. Next morning he arrived at White Stars with enough gowns to dress several weddings. James made himself scarce in token acceptance of custom, Zoe noted. It seemed strange, taking so much trouble over a wedding that was designed to self-destruct from the beginning. It was the only thought marring the preparations.

When Zoe broke the news to Genie, the little girl was beside herself with excitement. "Will you be Mrs. Boss?"

Zoe's laughter disguised the anguish provoked by the question. "No, sweetheart, I'll be Mrs. Langford."

"But James will be my really-truly daddy, won't he?"

He already was, Zoe thought with another pang. He had decided not to tell Genie the truth until they knew the outcome of the operation. It came to Zoe that she would finally achieve her heart's desire. For a brief time, she would be Genie's stepmother. The prospect gave her renewed strength for what lay ahead.

James had arranged everything with characteristic efficiency. On Friday morning his deputy, Brian Dengate, flew in by helicopter to be best man. Grace looked radiant as Zoe's matron of honor. After the reception the helicopter would take the newlyweds to Sydney to spend the night at a luxury hotel overlooking Sydney Harbor.

All that remained was the ceremony that would make them husband and wife.

Few places provided as romantic a setting for a wedding as White Stars, she thought as she prepared to make her entrance into the formal living room. It was lavishly decorated for the occasion with the furniture artfully rearranged around a center aisle. A veritable florist's shop of white roses filled the air with their seductive scent.

Restraining himself to an I-told-you-so look, Howard Leigh had gladly agreed to give her away and Zoe was grateful for the doctor's supportive arm. The walk toward the waiting celebrant seemed endless as she considered the enormity of what she had agreed to.

Then she looked at James and all doubts fled as she saw the certainty and purpose emanating from him like an aura. In his eyes she encountered something else, which awed her—an appreciation that made her feel like the most beautiful woman in the world.

She had never thought of herself as beautiful, and her parents hadn't encouraged such vanities. Her mother had even suggested she was lucky Andrew had married her, actually saying that few other men would have looked twice.

Now, seeing the soft glow of James's admiration, she knew her mother was wrong. James seemed unable to take his eyes off her as she moved slowly, gracefully toward him.

From the Gada collection she had chosen an ivory Thai silk jacket trimmed with seed pearls, worn over a dramatic sunray-pleated georgette skirt. Cream hosiery and silk-covered pumps completed the outfit.

Flower petals fluttered at her feet and she looked down to see Genie conscientiously strewing the bridal path with flowers from a tiny ribboned basket. The child looked enchanting in a pumpkin silk dress with puffed sleeves and satin sash, a garland of antique silk flowers in her hair. Only Zoe knew the persuasion it had taken to get Genie into the dress instead of her beloved riding clothes.

The smile that tilted the corners of her mouth at this thought brightened even more as she lifted her gaze back to James. He looked magnificent in a charcoal suit, white shirt and silk tie, the rich fabrics emphasizing his height and powerful build. *A man to be reckoned with,* she thought.

Her remaining apprehension was swept away by the sense of rightness that infused her as she took her place at his side. Later would be soon enough to examine her reasons, but for now she couldn't bring herself to regret what she was about to do.

"Do you, Zoe Elizabeth Holden, take James Matthew Langford..."

"I do." Astonishing how easily the words fell from her lips.

"Do you James Matthew Langford take Zoe Elizabeth Holden..."

"I do." His quiet assurance made her heart skip a beat.

Then it was done. She and James were married.

For better, for worse, for richer, for poorer. She was thankful he hadn't allowed the celebrant to include the traditional, "till death do us part" because it was all too possible that it could.

Knowing what he faced lent an urgency to her response when, at the celebrant's invitation, James bent to kiss the bride. As his mouth found hers she was swept away on a dizzying sense of being absorbed by him, taken into his very being, as if by marrying him, she had entered into a union more of the spirit than the flesh.

Her eyes closed as she struggled to deal with the flash flood of emotions raging through her, making it all but impossible to pull her thoughts into order. It was only a kiss for appearances' sake, yet it touched her heart and mind even as it imprinted her body.

Only one coherent thought remained: *What had she done?*

She was brought back to earth with a resounding crash as James released her and led her to a side table where the marriage certificate awaited their signature. Beside the document lay another one, several pages of fine print and to her dazed glance, a tangle of legalese.

"What is this?"

He brought his head closer so his words were for her alone. "Our agreement. I tried to have it simplified, but you know what lawyers are like. Basically it puts into black-and-white what we have already agreed, that we remain married for one month after my operation, after which, if I survive, we go our separate ways. In that event, it spells out the access you will have to Genevieve and the settlement you will receive in return for your help. You'll find it more than generous."

She went cold all over. From the transcendent wonder of his kiss to harsh reality, the transition was almost too much to absorb. She resisted an insane urge to hurl her wedding bouquet into his face and tell him she'd changed her mind. She couldn't go through with this after all. But it was already too late, they were legally married.

Somehow she got through the rest of the afternoon, giving the expected responses to the good wishes they were offered. The staff at White Stars had excelled themselves, providing a wedding buffet fit for royalty, but Zoe had no appetite for the food, however delicious. Signing the documents had brought the reality of the situation home to her much too forcibly.

Still it was an effort to tear her eyes away from the commanding figure moving so easily among the guests. It was hard to believe there was anything the matter with him, if you didn't count the strain that Zoe thought she saw settle around him like a cloud every time he thought he was unobserved.

Even then he presented a picture of rugged individualism. He was half a head taller than most of the men in the room but made no concessions to it, never stooping or rounding those impressive shoulders. He ate little and drank even less, Zoe noted, but socialized with his guests as if he had not a care in the world, far less a life-and-death struggle ahead of him. He was so incredibly virile that Zoe felt her throat dry every time she looked at the man she had just married.

"Relax, he won't disappear if you take your eyes off him," Julie said, sneaking up behind her.

Zoe summoned a tense smile. It was great to see Julie and her little boy again, even under these circumstances. "Still the incurable romantic, Julie?"

Her neighbor gave a deep sigh. "You'd think I'd learn, wouldn't you? I wonder if I'll ever find a man to love me the way James loves you. It's so obvious that I'm green with envy. You denied it, but I knew you two had something going the day you showed him that house at Strathfield."

Zoe wondered what Julie would make of the real situation between Zoe and James. The intense looks that blazed across the room between them possibly could be mistaken for love, if you didn't know that James was more concerned with Genie's future, than with Zoe's feelings. Still, it was hard to suppress the sense of yearning that gripped her whenever his vivid gaze locked with hers. If only they *were* looks of love. How different she would feel then.

Determinedly she shook off the half-formed desire. What was the point of wishing for the moon? Knowing she was doing this for Genie should be its own reward. Somehow the thought wasn't as comforting as it should have been.

Zoe felt rather than saw James appear at her elbow. Some psychic sense alerted her to his present moments before he said, "It's time for us to leave."

It was too soon and not nearly soon enough. They had agreed to spend their wedding night in Sydney to avoid fueling gossip about the nature of their marriage. From there, James would check into the hospital for his operation. It was hardly an ideal honeymoon, but it made a convenient cover story.

James had assured her all the legal formalities were in place, both for her and Genie to reside at White Stars and for the corporation to continue if the worst happened. He had also briefed Brian Dengate. Grace and her husband already knew about the situation. There was no one else who needed to be involved. It was all so matter-of-fact that Zoe wanted to scream. This was not some business deal. It was James's *life*.

She tried to tell herself she would feel the same way about anyone facing such an ordeal, but the thought lacked conviction. Had she begun to care about him at some level, and not only as Genie's father? No. She refused to allow herself to make such a stupid mistake.

By focusing her attention on getting ready to leave, she managed to subdue the troubling thought. Nevertheless, it simmered at the back of her mind as she exchanged her wedding dress for a rust-colored suit that she had chosen as her going-away outfit from the selection provided by Aloys Gada. James's staff had already transferred her luggage to the company helicopter that was going to take them to Sydney.

Even though she was outwardly ready, inwardly was another matter she thought as she rejoined James. Genie held tightly to his hand on the short walk to the helicopter pad. Zoe had already assured the little girl that they would only be gone for a few days, and that Grace would take good care of her. As a result, Genie seemed less upset by the coming separation than Zoe herself.

"Grace says I can try riding Amira without the leading rein next week. Isn't it great?" Genie enthused when Zoe bent down to hug her.

Zoe's hold tightened. "It's terrific, sweetheart. Just be careful for me, and be good for Grace."

"I will."

"Ready, Zoe?" Having said his own farewells, James strode toward the waiting helicopter. The rotor blades were already whipping up eddies of dust around the fringe of the landing pad.

Zoe felt torn. Grace was fond of Genie and having raised her own children, she was more than capable of taking care of her, but Zoe still had to steel herself to walk away. As Zoe took her seat beside James in the helicopter, he slid a hand into hers. "It isn't easy, is it?"

She gave him a wordless shake of her head, her vision blurring. His hold didn't slacken and she clung to him as they took off, watching the group on the ground until Genie was a white speck. Then she turned to James. "Was this how you felt when Ruth…" She couldn't go on around the lump filling her throat.

He gave a taut nod. "Yes."

The one-word answer made her heart ache. How had he borne it? Ruth hadn't even allowed him the luxury of a proper goodbye. For the first time she fully understood what the separation must have been like for him and a feeling of such savagery tore through her that she was shaken. How could Ruth have put him through such pain?

She saw him set himself to deal with the memory, then he gave a slight shudder as if to free himself of it. "Don't worry. Genevieve will have a great time with Grace. You can call them as often as you like."

She nodded distantly, aware that not all her concern was for Genie. "I know. I'm sure she'll be fine."

"But you're still unhappy. Not on my account, I trust?"

She was well aware that not caring was a condition of her marriage. James would be appalled at how much her thoughts had begun to revolve around him, especially now that they were officially husband and wife. Yet try as she might, she couldn't seem to stop them. "It's the helicopter. I've never liked them," she explained. Her work as a property manager had entailed occasional rides in them and they still made her feel uneasy. "I'll be okay once we get to the hotel."

He cleared his throat softly, drawing her eyes to his face. A slight smile turned up the corners of his mouth. "I hope you're more comfortable on a yacht than in a helicopter."

As his words sunk in, she drew a strangled breath. A yacht implied confined spaces, nowhere she could escape from James. Although why she felt the need to didn't bear close scrutiny. "We aren't going to a hotel?"

He shook his head. "The company's yacht is moored at Rushcutters Bay. It's comfortable and private."

Her heart hammered against her rib cage. She tried to tell herself her concern was for James's medical condition. "Is it safe for you? What if something goes wrong?"

"The yacht is equipped with radio and phone, and a full staff trained in first aid." Mild amusement colored his tone. "Are you sure that's your only problem, Zoe?"

"Of course. What else would it be?"

"What else, indeed?"

The yacht, *Harbor Knight*, was a fantasy vessel, a sleek futuristic-looking cruiser designed for luxury sailing, from the covered sundeck with its upholstered seating to a Jacuzzi on the foredeck, which could be filled with freshwater or saltwater.

High ceilings and cane furniture made the main deck light and airy. The dining room, bar and saloon could accommodate sixty passengers, James told her. Colors ranged from white to buttery cream, taking their inspiration from a Matisse print on the silk-covered wall. Even the door handles were custom-designed and included James's company crest.

She refused his invitation to inspect the staterooms, choosing instead to go up on deck and pretend interest in the harbor foreshores as they cruised around Cremorne and Mosman Bay, an oddly peaceful sanctuary with trees growing almost to the water's edge, despite its proximity to the city's center.

"I grew up in Cremorne," James told her, pointing out a modest apartment block well back from the waterfront. "Grace's family used to live next door. She and my sister went to school together."

Zoe tried to still the trembling his touch induced in her. "It sounds idyllic."

He frowned darkly. "It was until my father died. The man my mother married thought I should leave school and start earning my keep. In a way he did me a favor. I was so determined to ask my stepfather for nothing that I saved every cent I earned and invested it in property. I lived in one room and got by on one meal a day, but the first house I ever lived in, I owned."

"You must have been very lonely," she observed, thinking of her own childhood with her parents frequently absent on scientific expeditions and only her grandparents to provide any sort of home life. At least she'd had them. James had had no one.

"Don't waste your sympathy on me, Zoe. I did all right out of it. Remember the old saying, what doesn't destroy us makes us stronger."

If it was true, she'd be invincible when this was over, she thought, seriously doubting it. As the night drew in and the lights came on around the foreshores, turning the harbor waters into a diamond-strewn velvet surface, it was becoming harder to ignore the reality of her situation.

She was his wife. This was their wedding night. The yacht might indeed be staffed but the staff were almost invisible in their quiet efficiency. In the saloon, James had given her a tour of the built-in television and video equipment, but she was not in the mood for one of the yacht's vast library of movies on tape. So she sat beside him in the gathering dark, her awareness of him growing with the shadows.

What was he thinking about as he sat beside her in silence while the parade of ferries and pleasure craft, now mere garlands of lights, glided over the obsidian surface of the harbor? She found herself studying his profile, outlined strongly by the glow emanating from the saloon below. His lips were slightly parted, inviting her to remember the feel of them against her own. Beneath craggy brows his eyes were dark caverns, forbidding yet exciting in their mysteriousness. Both hands rested on his knees, which were slightly apart, his feet planted solidly against the decking, bracing his body against the gentle roll of the yacht with the tide.

She licked her lips, which had become dry suddenly, as a tendril of fierce sensation whipped through her, shocking in its intensity. The power of it almost brought her to her feet, every fiber of her being in revolt. He was an overwhelmingly attractive man. It was normal to feel the pull of such a powerful chemistry, especially given all that had passed between them today.

She had been on her own for a long time since Andrew died, not really wanting any serious involvement after the hell he had put her through. Now she was feeling the echoes of old needs and desires, revived by the emotional strain of the day. James was the catalyst, that was it.

"You're restless," he said out of the darkness. "Not regretting today?"

"Of course not. We have an agreement and I intend to honor it." Her voice sounded alarmingly shaky even to her own ears.

She tensed as he moved up behind her, his breath a soft wind against the sensitive nape of her neck. "Is there any reason why you can't enjoy it as well?"

Chapter Ten

As the dusk turned to dark James was well aware that Zoe was watching him. He wished he could read her mind. Was the same thought on her mind that was on his? This was their wedding night. But Zoe's stillness gave him no clue as to how she felt about it. Ruth had never been still and had never spent even a night aboard the yacht, claiming it made her feel too confined. Zoe didn't seem to mind.

But then she was very different from Ruth in ways he had only gradually begun to appreciate. It wasn't only her skills with Genevieve, admirable though they were. No, it was more an inner strength that had enabled her to survive her experience with her late husband and emerge stronger, wiser, unbowed in body or spirit.

Her strength drew James like a magnet, not only because she would need every bit of it if his operation went badly. If he was honest, there was another, more personal reason. At some level he recognized her spirit as the counterpart of something in himself, almost like the missing pieces of a puzzle. When he was around Zoe, he felt…complete. There was no other way to put it.

Crazy fool, he told himself impatiently. The prospect of the operation must be making him sentimental. Zoe had no time for him, only for his child whom she thought of as her own.

Sometimes there was no justice. As it was, her nearness made him increasingly aware of his manhood—and not especially comfortably, either. Why hadn't he booked them into a hotel where they would have had places to go and things to do other than focus on each other?

From the moment he brought Zoe aboard *Harbor Knight*, he knew he had made a mistake. He had chosen the yacht for peace and privacy, both of which he badly needed. But he had reckoned without the disturbing effect of Zoe herself on his peace of mind—and other parts of his anatomy. Knowing she was legally his wife only made it worse.

Why hadn't he noticed before how stunningly attractive Zoe was? Oh, he'd noted her good points almost from the first meeting—what red-blooded man wouldn't? But he hadn't allowed the total effect of the woman to fully impact on his consciousness until this moment. Out on the water with only the stars and the ghostly movements of other vessels for company, breathing in the delicate aura of her perfume, he felt his muscles tighten with the urge to pull her into his arms.

He'd never felt so off balance before, not even when he and Ruth were courting in the Middle East. Thrown together by circumstances, they'd clung together like people in the same life raft. Like people in that situation, they should have gone their separate ways as soon as the raft reached a safe shore. They probably would have done just that, if not for the accident that had left Ruth pregnant with his child.

In a million lifetimes, he could never regret Genevieve, but he did regret that he hadn't been able to give Ruth more of whatever she craved from life. It was certainly not him.

So he was right back where he started. Zoe was not Ruth, thank goodness, but she had about as much interest in him as a man as Ruth had. To Zoe he was an obstacle, the man standing between her and the child she adored.

He felt like a kid with his nose pressed against a candy store window. By marrying Zoe he had bought the store, but it was still locked against him. And he had effectively given her the keys as part of their deal. She would probably be horrified if she knew the direction his thoughts were taking.

A rush of breath caught his attention and he started guiltily. Had she somehow picked up on his thoughts? He watched her wrap her arms around herself as she drifted to the mahogany railing and leaned against it, staring into the water.

"Restless?" he asked her. When she nodded he moved up behind her, close enough to inhale the wonderful scent of her. It reminded him of the seductive jasmine fragrances used by the women of the East. "Not regretting today?"

The muscles in the back of her neck knotted and it was all he could do not to drop his hands to her shoulders and massage the tension away. If he touched her now, he knew he would be in big trouble. "We have an agreement and I intend to honor it," he heard her say stiffly. Something in her tone made him think it wasn't what she wanted to say at all.

Big trouble, he sighed to himself. His thoughts might be occupied with romance, but she was obviously taking a more pragmatic view, no doubt wondering how soon she could excuse herself and go to bed—alone.

"I know we have an agreement," he acknowledged heavily, not sure why he felt so disappointed. "But is there any reason why you can't enjoy it as well?"

In the golden light spilling from the saloon, he saw surprise flare in her expression. "I am enjoying myself. It's an idyllic spring evening. The water is like glass and the stars look close enough to touch.''

He could see stars, too, but his were in the eyes she turned to him and it was tempting to tell her so. If it wasn't for his previous experience with Ruth, he might have weakened and done so, but he and Zoe were as much under the gun now as he'd been before in the Middle East. Until the outcome of his surgery was known, there was no point in starting something he couldn't finish. Maybe if he lived through the next week, he would need to reconsider, but not now.

''It's getting cool,'' he said, taking her arm in as clinical a touch as he could manage. The slight contact still played havoc with his insides, but he mastered it by sheer force of will. ''Let's go below. The chef should have dinner ready by now.''

What was the matter with her? Zoe asked herself as James escorted her to the dining saloon where everything was ready for their dinner. For a moment, James sounded as if *he* was the one regretting their bargain. Was he so against being committed to her in marriage, even temporarily? After Ruth his wariness was understandable, but there was no need on Zoe's account. After Andrew, she'd had her fill of loveless marriages. She wasn't about to repeat the mistake, with or without the prenuptial agreement that James had made sure she signed.

He seated her on one of the cream-upholstered banquettes facing a wall of mirrors. In the reflection she saw him massage the back of his neck, a frown etching his tanned forehead. As he sat down opposite her she felt immediately remorseful. How could she think of herself at a time like this?

''Another headache?'' she asked.

He shrugged dismissively. "Nothing serious. Champagne?"

Following his lead she dropped the subject and deliberated between the Domaine Chandon and Perrier-Jouët vintages he offered, finally choosing the Australian-grown wine.

With fabulous flower arrangements, Felix Frères silver, Hutschenreuther 1814 china, Villeroy and Boch glassware and a menu worthy of a five-star restaurant, there were distractions aplenty, but still she found her eyes lingering on James between courses. The growing strain around his mouth and eyes wasn't lost on her, and she ached for a way to ease it. But how could she when he only wanted her help in securing Genie's future?

The fact soured her pleasure in the chef's magnificent offerings of ravioli filled with lobster mousse a la crème, followed by twin mignon of venison in cantaloupe cream. She refused dessert of coconut soufflé with Drambuie sauce, in favor of filtered coffee with a splash of fresh cream.

James also settled for coffee and leaned back, resting one long-fingered hand along the back of the banquette. "Would you like port or a liqueur to go with that?"

She shook her head. "Two glasses of champagne are already more than I usually have."

He smiled. "Then it's just as well you aren't driving home."

"No need to remind me," she said, strain sharpening her voice.

He studied her long and hard over the rim of his coffee cup. "Is it such a trial, being here with me?"

It was but not for the reasons he probably imagined. Ever since they came below, her body had started feeling like a tuning fork, awaiting the right touch to send it wild with vibrations. The dining saloon was spacious, but James still seemed far too close for comfort. Her breasts rose and fell in time with her ragged breathing, until she wondered if her knees would hold her without buckling if she stood up.

This would have to stop. She replaced the cup in its saucer. "I'm tired. Do you mind if I go to bed?"

A shadow fell across his rugged features. If she hadn't known better, she would swear he was disappointed. "I'll show you to your cabin."

"No, it's all right. Stay and finish your coffee. I'm sure I can remember the way."

Before he could insist on escorting her, she stumbled out of the main saloon and along the corridor that she recalled led to their staterooms. She had only peeked into the one James had chosen for her, before taking the coward's way out and heading up on deck. But she had seen that it was as large as a hotel suite, with its own bathroom and sitting area. On the way to her room she passed the door to his suite, the twin of hers.

By the time she closed her own door and leaned against it, her heart was beating a frantic tattoo. She was mature enough to know when she was aroused sexually, and this she was in spades. James was more of a man than any she had ever known and to be forced to spend an evening in such close quarters with him, she would need to be under a vow of chastity to remain unaffected.

But that wasn't the whole story. There was also an emotional tug that was completely unexpected and more powerful even than the siren song of his maleness. It pierced her heart with the need to be loved and cherished not as a prized possession, as she had been to Andrew, but as a soul mate in all things, sharing not only beds, but lives, in all their messy, roller-coaster diversity.

Alarmed by the trend of her thoughts, she went into the bathroom, snapping on lights as if it would help to shed light on her own foolish notions. The impossibly flattering mirror refused to reveal anything but glowing skin, wide, bright eyes and tousled blond curls as she dipped her head and splashed cooling water onto her hot features. Lined up under the mirror was a Rodeo Drive cosmetics selection of Mary Chess soap, Rene Guinot sun lotion and Tova 9 shampoo, but no potions to deal with what she was afraid *really* ailed her.

Was she starting to care for James?

No, no, no. Everything in her protested at the idea. Hadn't she learned anything from her marriage to Andrew? A loveless marriage was hell on earth, and she didn't intend to endure it ever again. She accepted that James was totally different from Andrew. He was far more generous and compassionate, with a heart as big as the man himself for one thing. But James was no more in love with her than Andrew had been.

James's motives were certainly more salutary. He wanted to assure Genie's future no matter what happened to him, which was why Zoe had agreed to the union. But when all was said and done, both he and Andrew had married her for their own reasons. Love had nothing to do with it.

Zoe dried her face on the fluffy towel then returned to the bedroom determined to blank the whole agonizing problem out of her mind and settle to sleep. The emotionally draining day had exhausted her and the queen-size bed beckoned in its curtained alcove. A maid had turned the covers down during dinner, making it look even more inviting.

With the shimmering folds of her Thai silk nightdress poised over her head, Zoe paused, wondering whether she was also in James's thoughts. It *was* their wedding night after all. The coffee-colored fabric whispered down over her body in the palest imitation of a caress and she shuddered involuntarily. Putting him out of her mind was going to be easier said than done.

So it proved when she slid between the crisp, mono-grammed sheets. The moment she closed her eyes he in-vaded her mind, his azure eyes sparkling and his wonder-fully mobile mouth curved into a soul-wrenching smile. You want him, said a voice in her heart. No matter what the terms of this marriage, James is your husband. He's a powerfully attractive man. It's normal to want him. It would be abnormal not to.

To want him or to love him?

The question reverberated so strongly through her mind that she realized she had asked it out loud. Her eyes snapped open. Oh God, had she done the unthinkable by falling in love with James?

It would explain so many things: the powerful pull he exerted over her emotions; the yearnings, which twisted her into knots whenever he was in the same room; the mortal dread she felt for what he was facing. She was in love with James Langford. It was as basic and inescapable as that. Given the way he felt about her, she was probably the big-gest fool in the whole, wide world.

Although she burrowed deeper into the bed, she couldn't turn off the voice in her heart, no matter how much her head told her she ought to. She didn't want to turn it off if the truth be told. What she really wanted to do hardly bore thinking about.

So why was she sitting up and reaching for the negligee that matched her nightgown? Why was she thrusting her bare feet into soft slippers and padding toward the cabin door? She was only going to the galley to make herself some herbal tea, she told herself. The strong coffee with which she had finished her meal was keeping her awake.

By the time she reached the galley she had almost con-vinced herself it was true. Then she came across the last bottle of champagne James had opened. It sat in a silver ice bucket on the table, apparently overlooked by the crew when they'd cleared away the dinner things. Or else they had left it in case James decided to have a final glass before turning in. Dewdrops of moisture ran down the sides of the bottle like tears.

She regarded it in torn silence for several minutes as she struggled to reach a decision. Once opened, champagne cannot be resealed. It has to be enjoyed in all its bubbly splendor, or not at all.

Like the marriage between her and James.

Fate had given them this one night as man and wife. Next week if the operation was a success, he would have no further use for Zoe. If he died—she almost choked on the terrifying thought, but it had to be faced. If he died, he would also be lost to her. This was a night out of time. If she let it go by without acting on the impulse, which grew stronger by the moment, she would probably regret it for the rest of her life.

No matter what James felt for her, she loved him and she wanted to show him in the only way that would have any real meaning. If he died, she would always have the memory of this night. If he lived, she would still have the memory. In either case—and the thought almost stopped her heart—it was all she would have. But it would be better by far than regrets.

He wasn't entirely immune to her. Tonight he had behaved as if he was attracted to her, she would swear to it. The way his eyes kept straying to her whenever he thought himself unobserved, and the beguiling way he made excuses to touch her. Perhaps she was seeing what she wanted to see, but perhaps not.

What she would do if James insisted on keeping to their bargain of a marriage of convenience, she refused to think about. The cork was well and truly out of the bottle. By tomorrow, the sparkle would be gone. Before she could change her mind, she scooped the champagne out of the ice bucket, swathed it in a white linen napkin and tucked it under her arm. Between the fingers of her free hand she slid the stems of two crystal flutes.

Her heart hammered so loudly she was surprised the sound didn't wake the crew as she retraced her steps along the corridor, stopping this time at the door to James's suite. The faintest trace of light glimmered underneath the door. He was still awake.

Rearranging her burdens, she freed a hand to knock on the cabin door. Her legs felt weak and she shivered, although the air-conditioning made it impossible for her to be cool, even in her flimsy nightwear.

"Who is it?" came James's vibrantly baritone response to her knock, which sounded far less confident than she had intended.

She tightened her hold on the champagne bottle. There was no going back now. In a few moments she would find out whether she had misjudged James's response to her this evening. She knew she had not misjudged her own to him. But it still took all the courage she possessed to say calmly, "It's your wife."

Chapter Eleven

"Zoe?" James looked stunned when he opened the door
to her. Her heart turned over. He had shed his white shirt,
and his pants rode low on narrow hips. A towel was slung
around his neck. In the pool of light spilling from the cabin,
his naked torso shone as if bronzed. A fine scattering of
dark chest hair arrowed downward, disappearing beneath
his belt line. Her throat dried as she took in the signs that
she had interrupted his preparations for bed.

"Couldn't you sleep?" he asked, sounding much more
hoarse than he had a moment before.

Barely able to speak, she shook her head and held out
the champagne flutes. "I thought maybe a nightcap..."

To her chagrin he forestalled her entry into his cabin by
angling his substantial body across the opening. "This isn't
a good idea, Zoe. You said yourself you've had more than
your usual quota of champagne."

"It was only two glasses," she insisted, appalled that he
should connect her presence at his door with an excess of
alcohol. Had she been completely wrong about the signals

he'd been sending her, allowing her own needs to override common sense? "You're probably right, it isn't a good idea after all."

She turned away, intending to escape to her own cabin as quickly as she could and attempt to erase the whole mortifying scene from her mind, but his hand came crashing down on her shoulder. "Not so fast."

"But you just said—"

"I said it isn't a good idea. I didn't say I had a problem with it."

The heat of his gaze bored all the way to her core, threatening imminent meltdown. This was a monumental mistake. He didn't love her. He didn't even want her here now. The wedding night she had lain awake imagining was no more than a fantasy, borne of her own yearnings.

She knew she should retreat, but her feet refused to track. Her skin flushed as if she had a fever. It *was* a fever, but of the blood. And the only cure she could conceive of stood in front of her, his hand resting possessively on her shoulder.

The deck shifted beneath her feet, throwing her against him. Reflex made him wrap his arms around her. He held the pose for a heartbeat then his mouth fastened on hers, whirling her into a maelstrom of sensations so powerful that they swept away all rational thought.

With a muffled oath, he drew her into the cabin, taking the bottle and glasses from her in the next fluid movement. The cabin door swung with the yacht's gently rolling motion and he kicked it shut before pulling her into his arms again.

This time his kiss was a more leisurely voyage of exploration, but still it battered at the rapidly crumbling walls of her self-control. The cabin reeled around her and she linked both arms around his neck, the better to keep her balance, although whether internal or external, she wasn't sure.

She only knew she loved James. The discovery was new enough to fill her with astonishment as well as an anguish that reached to the depths of her being. It was the cruelest irony that he had set as his sole condition for marriage that she *not* love him. It might be possible for James, whose heart plainly wasn't involved, but she might as well order the sea to stop foaming against the shore. It would be about as effective as ordering herself not to care.

She held to the consolation that he didn't know how she felt. With the life-and-death challenge ahead of him, he didn't need the added complication of her love, only the assurance that his daughter's future was secured. Letting him believe she was content with their bargain was the least Zoe could do for him.

Knowing that the memory of this night would have to last her a long, long time lent an urgency to her responses that left her shaken. "Is something wrong?" he asked, leaning back a little to appraise the paleness she felt but couldn't conceal. His concern darkened the brilliant blue of his eyes.

With the clarity of her newly heightened emotions, she was aware of everything about him, from the enticing way a curl of dark hair fell across his forehead, to the slightly abrasive feel of his torso through the thin silk of her nightgown and the heat of his hands searing her lower back as he cupped her to him. A shadow of beard smudged the strong line of his chin. His last shave must have been hours ago, but her sharpened senses caught the lingering tang of the aftershave lotion he had used.

"Nothing's wrong," she said in a voice barely above a whisper, and knew it was no lie. At this moment, in his arms, everything was exquisitely, gloriously right. His kisses seemed to come from some deep emotional wellspring, which made her heart leap as she answered them from her own depths.

"If you want me to stop, you'd better tell me now, while it's still an option," he offered, his mouth only a breath away from hers. "This wasn't part of our agreement."

Bitter disappointment lanced through her, although he was only voicing what she had told herself before coming to his cabin. From the beginning he had offered her marriage for one purpose only—to protect the child they both loved. He hadn't asked for her love and was not offering his now, only a night of shared physical pleasure, which he assumed was what she wanted, too.

And she did, pity help her. Whatever happened in the future, she wanted the sweet memory of this night. "I don't want you to stop," she breathed into the hollow of his shoulder where she had rested her head as her thoughts whirled.

His arm came under her knees, lifting her so she was cradled against the unyielding wall of his chest. Her arm dropped around his shoulder and her fingers grazed the puckered skin where the terrorist's bullet had penetrated. An arrow pierced her heart as she imagined him hurt, or worse. "You shouldn't carry me," she protested. "You'll aggravate your injury."

"Not touching you will aggravate it a lot worse," he growled. They had reached the bed, so the question became academic as he set her gently down in the curtained alcove. Her negligee fell open and he dragged in a deep breath as his eyes went to the soft swell of her breasts outlined by the low-cut nightdress. "You're like a vision out of a dream," he murmured.

Her throat closed. Andrew had looked at her with the satisfaction of a collector admiring his prized exhibit. The look on James's face was more akin to worship. Never had she felt more beautiful or desirable. With a tiny sigh, she stretched out her arms and he slid onto the bed beside her. One hand threaded through her hair as he rained kisses across her face and throat, while the other pressed against the bone of her hip, lifting her against him until the wild pounding of his heart throbbed through her own body.

When he slid her nightgown off her shoulders to caress the warm fullness of her breasts, her remaining control spun away in a whirlpool of desires she could barely begin to identify. His lips skimmed across her heated skin, eliciting a shudder of pure pleasure. This was where she belonged, in the arms of the man she loved.

The sensation of his mouth exploring every inch of her bared skin was as intoxicating as the finest wine and she drank deeply, inhaling the masculine feel and touch and taste of him until she was dizzy with yearnings only James could possibly satisfy.

When he flung one muscular leg across hers, the hard perfection of his body met her softness in miraculous accord. Joyfully she opened her arms to enfold him, resenting even her whisper-thin gown as a barrier between them. She trembled with a longing so powerful it shook her to her core.

At her tremors, he opened heavy-lidded eyes and smiled reassurance deep into hers but his breathing was as labored as her own. Her heart soared. Whatever the future held for them, he would never forget this night any more than she could or would. She closed her eyes and gave herself up to the sheer ecstasy of his touch.

Suddenly James's shoulders spasmed and she jerked her eyes open, shocked to see that his face was ashen. "What is it? What's the matter?"

He bit down on his lower lip and she could see the effort it cost him even to shake his head. "It's just a twinge. It will pass in a second."

It had to, she thought desperately. How could she stand seeing him like this? There had to be something she could do. She slid off the bed and helped him to lie down on it.

It was a measure of his suffering that he didn't try to resist. He lay back with his eyes closed, his jaw clenching until the veins stood out in his neck.

With a soft groan he passed out altogether and her heart turned to stone inside her. The fingers she pressed to his neck found a pulse that was alarmingly thready. No, it couldn't end like this.

She ran to alert the crew.

She prayed as she had never prayed before as the yacht put in at Cremorne Wharf where James, still unconscious, was transferred to a waiting ambulance. "I'm coming with you," she told the paramedics as they worked on him. "I'm his wife," she added, her look daring them to raise a single objection.

One look at her face convinced them because they made room for her without demurral. During the yacht's dash to the wharf she had thrown on a pair of jeans and a sweater but her tousled hair and flushed face must have told their own story. Not that she cared if the whole world knew she had been in James's bed when he collapsed. Her only concern right now was for the man she loved. If he had been alone when the attack hit...

Her blood chilled as another possibility struck her. Had she contributed to the attack by coming to him tonight? It was a profitless line of thought. She couldn't undo what had happened. All she could do was cling to his hand, trying to infuse some of her strength into him as they raced through the city streets, lights and sirens clearing their path, until they reached the hospital.

Notified by radio, a team of specialists was waiting for them headed by James's surgeon who introduced himself as Bill Margolin. He swiftly checked James over then gave a string of instructions to his team. While they carried out his orders, the surgeon sought out Zoe, hovering white-faced outside the emergency room. "I believe you were with him when he collapsed."

She nodded, wrapping her arms around herself. "Will he be all right?"

"No way to tell until I operate, but James is strong so there's every reason to hope for the best," he told her guardedly. "Are you a close relative?"

A pang shot through her as she saw the surgeon reach the same conclusion as the paramedics, that she was simply James's companion for the night. There was some small satisfaction in saying quietly, "I'm his wife. Tonight was our wedding night."

The doctor looked startled. "His wife? Surely James wouldn't—"

"He told me about the operation before we married," she forestalled him, "including the risk that he might not survive it."

Dr. Margolin regarded her with renewed respect. "You must love him a great deal to put yourself through this."

She did and the only one who didn't—couldn't—know it was James himself. "How long will it be until we know the outcome of the operation?" she asked shakily.

His frank gaze met hers. "Almost at once. If he comes around, the headaches will be gone and he'll have full mobility back."

He didn't need to spell out the alternative. For an instant she went cold, imagining it, before thrusting it from her mind. James would be all right. She wouldn't consider any other possibility.

She was shown to a private lounge to wait. The knot of tension inside made her want to scream, but there was nothing to do except leaf blindly through magazines, drink endless cups of coffee and resist the urge to pace. The specter of James unconscious in her arms refused to leave her.

"Oh God, let him be all right," she prayed, wanting the miracle more than she had ever wanted anything in her life.

She knew now why she had agreed to marry him. It was as much for her own sake as for Genie's. Some part of her had known she was lost from the moment he arrived on her doorstep in Sydney, although it had taken her weeks to accept it. All that he was called to her at some primeval level and her heart could do nothing but answer.

The time ticked by relentlessly, squeezing her emotions into a vise so tight she could hardly breathe. She paced. She drank more coffee. She leafed through magazines without seeing a word on the pages. At some point she must have dropped into an exhausted doze because she awoke when a hand flexed on her shoulder. "Mrs. Langford?"

It took her a moment to connect the unfamiliar name with herself then she jolted upright, fear clenching a tight fist around her heart. "James?"

Dr. Margolin frowned. "He came through the surgery with flying colors, but we're having trouble bringing him out of the anesthetic. He doesn't seem to want to wake up."

James had come so far. He couldn't give up now. "Will it help if I talk to him?"

He nodded. "Exactly what I was going to suggest."

She followed the surgeon into the recovery room and her heart constricted at the sight of James lying still and pale amid a tangle of tubes and monitors. She squared her shoulders. Whether he knew it or not, he wasn't alone in this battle. Afterward there would be no place for Zoe in his life, but for now she was his wife and would fight for him to the gates of hell and beyond if necessary. She met the doctor's eyes resolutely. "What do you want me to do?"

"Talk to him, sing to him, whatever you think will reach him. He's being monitored and the sister is right outside if you need anything."

The door closed behind the surgeon, leaving her alone

with James, the heavy silence punctuated by the discreet beeping of the medical equipment. Dragging a chair alongside the bed, she took James's hand and searched her mind for the right words to reach him. "It's Zoe," she began, her voice strengthening as inspiration came to her. "The doctor tells me the operation was a success. He removed the bullet and there's no nerve damage, so you won't have any more headaches or muscle weakness. You'll be your old virile self again." She almost choked on the word as it conjured up vivid images of being in his arms.

Tears threatened to brim over and she gulped them back. James needed her strength. Later would be soon enough to deal with her own struggles. "Come on, James," she went on, "surely you won't give in and let *me* win? If you die, I get sole custody of Genie, you hear? Genie. It's not what you want, is it? If you come back, I lose everything. Even you." It wasn't what she planned to say, but she couldn't prevent the admission from slipping out.

Her face was wet but her voice was strong as she added, "I know you don't love me, but I don't give you permission to go. You see…" Her voice broke on the admission she was powerless to hold back. "I love you." It was wrung from her so softly she prayed it wouldn't reach James where he was. Blindly she turned and shouldered her way out of the room.

She muttered an apology to the surgeon as she fled past him at the nurses' station. If she didn't get away, she knew she would break down completely, and what good would she be to James then?

She didn't stop until she reached the hospital chapel, a serene oasis of polished timber and stained glass, belonging to no denomination, yet providing a welcome to all. Thankfully the room was deserted at this hour. Zoe threw herself onto a seat, huddling into herself, more alone and afraid than she had ever felt. She had never allowed herself to think of James making anything but a full recovery. Even if she couldn't be with him, she wanted it for him desperately. If it was possible to will a man to live, she did it now, but she was terrified that it wouldn't be enough.

"Mrs. Langford?"

Zoe lifted her head and recognized James's nurse. Fear struck deep into her heart. "James, is he—"

The woman's face creased into a smile. "He's finally conscious. Dr. Margolin sent me to find you. He knew you'd want to see your husband right away."

Zoe nodded, too overwhelmed with relief to speak. She had no idea how much time had passed, but her limbs ached when she stood up to follow the nurse.

James was propped up a little higher, his blue eyes aware but flecked with weariness, she saw as she crossed to his bedside, her heart pounding. "I'm glad you're awake."

James did not return the pressure of her mouth when she leaned across to kiss him. "Bill says you were here all night." He didn't sound pleased about it.

"I wanted to be." Needed to be was probably more accurate, but she didn't think he would want to hear that.

She glanced at the doctor. "Is everything all right?"

Dr. Margolin grinned, an answer in itself. "Ask your husband. All he needed to bring him around was a word from his beautiful new wife."

James impaled him with a look. "Whose bright idea was that? Yours?"

The doctor nodded. "Worked, didn't it? I'll leave you two alone to talk. You'd better tell your wife the good news, James. She's had enough of the bad for one night." He ushered the nurse out of the door ahead of him.

"What good news does he mean?" she asked, twisting her hands together in front of her. She ached to have James wrap his arms around her so she could feel the pulse of his strong, healthy heart resonate through her own body. But he gave no sign that he wanted it so she stayed beside the bed, not touching him.

James waited until the door closed behind the doctor and nurse. "Bill means I'll make a complete recovery. But it's hardly good news for you, is it, Zoe?"

Tension crawled up the back of her neck. "Why wouldn't it be?"

"It would solve your problem. With me out of the way, you'd have Genevieve to yourself, not to mention a substantial fortune."

"I love Genie and I did want her with me," she admitted, "but I've seen how close she's become to you and how much she loves White Stars. Her welfare comes first."

"So you're leaving as we agreed?"

It was so obviously what he wanted that she nodded dumbly, lifting her head and blinking rapidly before he glimpsed her damp eyes. "How long will it be before you're fit enough to go home?"

His mouth twisted into a wry smile. "Bill says I'll be out of here in a few days." His head fell back against the pillow, his face going white. "You won't have to play the devoted bride for long, if that's what's bothering you."

"What else could it be?" She whirled out of the room and didn't look back even when she heard him call her name.

James moved restively. His head ached abominably, but the doctor said it was the aftereffects of the anesthetic. The pain didn't compare with the headaches he'd endured before the operation so he counted his blessings.

One of them plainly wasn't his new wife, he thought angrily. What had Bill meant about James needing Zoe to bring him around after the operation? Surely she'd have been happier if he died, yet she seemed almost glad he'd made it. Personally he was glad as hell he'd made it. He hadn't wanted to admit how scared he was of having the bullet removed. Everything happening so swiftly, there was no time to work himself into a cold sweat.

Zoe had been the one to sweat, which he hadn't intended. Maybe what he was reading as concern for him was really relief that it was over, so she could return to her old life. She hadn't denied it when he mentioned their agreement.

Somewhere in his mind lingered an image of her sitting by his bedside, holding his hand. What had she said? Something about her winning if he died. That was it. She had dared him to live and deprive her of her victory.

Well, he had taken her dare and lived. But something else nagged at him. He passed a hand across his clammy forehead. What in blazes was it?

His mind felt foggy. It was an effort to think straight, but he made himself focus. Then he had it. While he floated just below the level of consciousness, she'd said something about loving him.

The semiconscious mind was tricky. He couldn't trust impressions gained in such a state, but he could swear she'd said she loved him. The hell of it was, he didn't know whether it was a dream or a lie. Come to think of it, he didn't know which he'd prefer to deal with.

The dream was understandable, given the intoxicating way Zoe had felt in his arms. Remembering how she had come to his cabin in the night made him smile, but the expression vanished as he recalled how the terrorist's bullet had cheated him of the chance to make love to her. Did she regret whatever pity or duty had brought her to his cabin? Now that she knew he was going to live, she seemed anxious to cut the ties binding them.

So the lie was the more likely explanation. If it wasn't for Genevieve, Zoe would never have come to White Stars or agreed to be his wife. She did what was right, no matter what it cost her. Her loyalty to her first husband and her behavior toward Genevieve was ample proof.

James slammed one fist into the palm of the other. No matter how tempted he was—and he had to admit, he was sorely tempted—he would *not* have her stay with him out of some misguided sense of duty. He'd experienced one marriage like that and it was enough for a lifetime. If she wanted to leave, she had the right. He wouldn't stop her.

If she wanted to leave.

It was something he had a month to discover.

Chapter Twelve

Gradually the dense olive-clad escarpments of the Watagan State Forest gave way to the rolling hills and valleys of White Stars. From their vantage point in James's helicopter Zoe could pick out the avenue of hundred-year-old oak trees leading to the homestead.

There were more than fifty stables and a hundred paddocks and from the air she could identify the gleam of whitewash on the post-and-rail fences. On this sunny spring day, four stallions warily watched their approach from a ridge-top.

Her breathing quickened as the two-storeyed Georgian stone house came into view. She was home. Not at White Stars, of course, but in this beautiful area where she had spent the summers with her grandparents, in the only true home she could remember.

While James recovered in the hospital, she had reached some decisions of her own. She had resigned from her job as a property manager and prevailed on her old boss to help her find a suitable tenant for her house in Sydney. The rent would help pay the mortgage while she rented a place in the nearby town of Cooranbong, gateway to the Watagan area. She would be close enough for Genie to visit while living in the place that had claimed her heart as a teenager. For someone with her skills there was plenty of work even in the country. Her boss's glowing reference practically guaranteed her a job locally.

There would be sadness, too. Living close by she would have frequent reminders of her brief marriage to James. But as Genie's father there was no escaping him, no matter where she lived, so it might as well be somewhere she loved. Maybe in time she would be able to meet James without being assailed by an avalanche of painful yearnings every time he looked at her.

And pigs might fly, she thought bleakly. She twisted the simple gold wedding band which James had placed on her ring finger. Folklore once had it that a vein led from that finger straight to the heart. In her case it was true.

She flickered a glance at James, her heart tightening painfully. He looked a picture of commanding virility. Only the dressing visible beneath the collar of his polo shirt and a certain whiteness around his eyes hinted at the battle he had waged with death and won. He had won her, too, although he wasn't to know how irrevocably. It was her secret alone, the desperate longings he stirred in her. Her greatest regret was that he hadn't finished what he started on their wedding night.

He sat in brooding silence, his vivid eyes focused on the country beneath them, probably assessing the condition of his horses, and the work to be done. During the past week he'd seethed with plans for a future, which, before the operation, was frighteningly uncertain. No longer. He was back in charge and it showed.

She swallowed the lump clogging her throat as the pilot

set the helicopter down on the pad. "Looks like Grace drew the short straw," James murmured.

Zoe saw the stud manager waiting beside the four-wheel-drive vehicle. If she knew Grace, it was no chore to come for James. His bond with his staff made them practically family.

As such, the woman knew better than to fuss. "Glad to see you back in one piece, boss," she said pragmatically, but her eyes never left James until he was settled in the car with the luggage stowed in the back. Her warm smile included Zoe. "Hope you don't mind, but the team has organized a welcome-home barbecue for you tonight."

It was probably the last thing James wanted, but he smiled. "We'll cope."

If he had hoped for a quiet affair, he had underestimated his own popularity. Not only the White Stars staff but many of their neighbors turned up, curious to meet James's new wife as well, Zoe suspected. She wondered how he would explain her departure when the time came.

She noticed the quiet joy with which he introduced Genie as his daughter. Since the wedding the little girl had slipped easily into the role, and there was a definite ring of pride in the way she called him Daddy. Her welcome to Zoe was warmly affectionate, but it wasn't long before she gravitated back to James's side where she stuck like glue for most of the evening. No one knew yet that Genie was his daughter in fact as well as through his marriage to Zoe, but it was plain to Zoe that the truth couldn't make Genie love James any more than she did already.

Despite her inner turmoil Zoe had to admit the home paddock provided a glorious setting for a barbecue with its spring-fed dam fringed by tall gum trees, which scented the air with their fragrance. Through the trees, the red-gold of the setting sun looked like a forest fire. Overhead, a wedge-tailed eagle wheeled high in the sky, its wingspan as wide as the gravel road ringing the homestead.

There was a seemingly endless supply of food from hefty T-bone steaks to stuffed mushrooms as large as saucers, a dozen varieties of salad and freshly baked damper as well as rivers of Hunter Valley wine, beer and soft drinks.

Grace's husband, Jock, took charge of barbecuing the steaks. He had the square shoulders of a practiced horseman, with serious gray eyes and a full, slightly red beard. He moved rather stiffly and Grace told Zoe he had been a horse-breaker in his youth, suffering broken shoulders and a crushed chest. "He can't do as much around the property as he used to, but James won't hear of replacing him," Grace went on. "The boss is a special man, not that I'm telling you anything."

He *was* special to Zoe, if not in the way Grace meant. Zoe felt her throat close and her eyes mist, glad when Grace's attention was demanded elsewhere. She jumped as a man materialized out of the shadows beside her. It was Howard Leigh.

Concern speared through Zoe as she saw James with the doctor. "Is everything all right?"

Howard glanced at James. "If your husband gets any fitter, Bill Margolin and I will be out of business. I'm here strictly socially."

"You could have fooled me," James observed caustically.

Her eyebrow lifted and the doctor grinned. "He's grizzling because I told him to stay off those Arabian horses until that wound heals." He waggled a finger at James. "No contact sports or anything with a risk of impact or jarring. I'm relying on you to see he obeys doctors' orders, Zoe."

"I can try." Only she knew how little actual influence she possessed.

"And you," the doctor went on, spearing James with a look, "listen to your pretty new wife."

James shook his head. "Listening to her isn't what I had in mind."

The doctor made a noise of frustration. "Go easy on that, as well. Or take it slowly."

James's gaze locked with hers. "We will. Very slowly."

Her pulses thundered and her palms grew damp as she wrenched her gaze away. The doctor left, muttering to himself and she swung on James. "Did you have to suggest to Howard that I...that we..."

James shrugged. "I doubt if I said anything you weren't thinking."

Could he possibly know what had been on her mind since that night aboard the yacht? She took refuge in defiance. "How do you know what I'm thinking?"

"You have the most expressive face I've ever seen. Never, ever take up poker."

She felt a blush starting and not only because of what he'd implied in front of the doctor. James had divined her thoughts too accurately for comfort. She did want him. She loved him as she knew now she had never loved Andrew. How on earth was she going to live without James?

"I'd better find Genie. It's time she was in bed," she stammered.

His gaze softened. "I could say the same for her mother."

Had James been drinking? He didn't look like it, but he had been different somehow since they returned to White Stars. If she hadn't known better, she would have thought he *wanted* a real marriage. She caught herself in the vagrant wish that it could be so, then shook it off. What was the point of wishing for the moon?

Where else would Genie be but down at the stables, proudly introducing a neighbor's son to her horse, Amira?

Her reluctance to go to bed was obvious, but she complied with minimal grumbling. They were all tired after the long, emotionally draining day, and it didn't help that the party looked set to continue for some time.

Genie was subdued as Zoe helped her to wash and change into her nightgown. "Is something the matter?" she asked as she tucked the child into bed.

Genie's hold tightened on her favorite teddy bear, her small face puckering. "Don't you like James anymore?"

Pain closed around Zoe's heart. "We're good friends. What makes you think I don't like him?"

"You told Daddy you're going away," Genie said, tears welling in her expressive eyes. "I don't want you to go. I love you."

Zoe closed her eyes, fighting shock. Genie must have overheard her talking with James after they'd returned from Sydney earlier today. Zoe recalled saying something about going away, but she hadn't dreamed that Genie was within earshot. She cast about for a response that wasn't an outright lie. "You'll always have James. He's your daddy now and for always."

Genie sniffled. "I want you to be my mummy, too. Why can't you?"

Close to tears herself, Zoe gathered the child in a tight hug. "We can't always have what we want, sweetheart, but I'll always be your special friend. Is that better?"

"I 'spose so." Genie sounded reassured although her eyes remained teary. Then she forced a smile. "Guess what? I can ride Amira by my own self, without Grace holding the leading rein."

"Yes, she told me. I'm very proud of you." Grace had also said it was only within the training paddock with Grace herself hovering close by. "Sleep tight now. I love you."

"I love you, too," came the sleepy rejoinder. Not sure where she got the strength, Zoe tiptoed out of the room without breaking down. She knew she should probably rejoin the party, but she had no heart for it after her conversation with Genie.

Tomorrow she would have to talk to James. It seemed pointless to drag their marriage out for any longer when it had served its purpose. The longer she stayed, the harder her departure would be on everyone, especially herself.

Zoe found herself immersed in a nightmare where James and Genie walked ahead of her down some dark passageway. Try as she might, she couldn't catch up with them, nor did they turn when she called their names. Then they disappeared around a corner, leaving her alone.

The loneliness stayed with her when she struggled awake. She hadn't expected to sleep at all, far less well into the morning. Nor did she feel rested, the sense of desolation persisting as she rose and dressed in jeans and a pale blue silk shirt for what could be her last full day at White Stars.

When she went downstairs, the house was quiet. Few signs of the party remained. Genie's bed was neatly made, Zoe noticed as she passed the child's room. James must have gotten her out of bed and dressed, then taken her down to breakfast without waking Zoe. When she passed the study door, James was involved in what sounded like a business discussion on the phone so their talk would have to wait. Food was the last thing she wanted, but she headed for the kitchen in search of coffee.

She was brooding over a cup when Grace burst into the kitchen, her normally placid expression panicky. "Is James around?"

"In the study. What's the..." But Grace barreled past her without stopping. After a hurried conversation, which carried through the house, she and James came back into the kitchen together. His set expression triggered alarm bells in Zoe's head. "What's wrong?"

"Genevieve's gone riding on Amira."

Panic flared through Zoe. "By herself?"

Grace wrung her hands. "She was holding the pony's reins while I led Ferrere out for his morning exercise. I was only gone a couple of minutes. I still don't know how she managed to scramble up on the pony by herself, but they were gone when I came out. Someone must have left a gate unlatched after the party last night."

"Are you sure one of the stable hands didn't go with her?" James asked in a clipped voice. His face was a stone mask but his hands were clenched to white-knuckle tightness.

Grace shook her head, looking desperate. "I'm positive. None of them saw her ride off."

Zoe's heart raced. "Last night she told me she could ride Amira without a leading rein."

"Only in the training paddock under my supervision," Grace asserted. "I'd never let her go off by herself."

Zoe caught James's arm, feeling the hardness of set muscles under her fingers. It was tempting to hold on to him as to a lifeline, but she made herself let go. "There's something else you ought to know." She glanced at Grace, then took a deep breath. It was going to come out anyway, and it might be important under the circumstances. "Last night Genie was upset because she overheard me talking about going away."

James's hard gaze raked her and he swore quietly. "Then this is no accident." To Grace, he said, "I'll go after her on Ferrere. You check out the river flats. I'll scout along the ridge. She can't have gone far."

At the mention of his massive black stallion, Zoe went cold, the memory of her nightmare flooding back. She was terrified for Genie's safety and now she might risk losing both of them. His doctors had warned James against riding so soon after his surgery. "Can't you send some of the hands out?'' she implored, fear threading her voice. ''Dr. Leigh said you shouldn't ride while you're still healing.''

''Dr. Leigh doesn't have a four-year-old daughter lost in the wilderness,'' he snapped back.

His face said he wouldn't be stopped. She drew what courage she could from his determination and nodded reluctant assent. ''I'll come with you.''

He shook his head. ''Someone should stay here in case the horse brings her home.'' He touched a hand under her chin. ''Don't worry, I'll find her.''

Her shining eyes telegraphed the depth of her feelings for him. He would probably think it was for Genie, but the thought of the risk he was taking was all the more terrifying because she loved him so much. ''James, wait,'' she said urgently. ''I want to tell you—''

He stilled, watching her intently. ''Tell me what, Zoe?''

Pride made her withhold the admission. ''Just…be careful,'' she amended. He nodded tautly, then strode outside. Through the window she saw him swing himself onto the huge black stallion. As he aimed the horse toward the ridge, she wanted to beg him to take her with him, anything but let him ride off alone. But all she could do was wait.

Chapter Thirteen

At the sound of footsteps on the verandah her heart leapt but it was only Jock McGovern, wanting to make sure she was all right. "It's damned frustrating not to be able to go after them," he growled. His old injuries made riding impossible these days. "In the old days I'd have ridden after them like a shot."

An idea seized her. "You can't, but maybe I can. If you'll wait in the house, I can take the four-wheel-drive."

Jock regarded her keenly. "Do you think the wee lass has headed for Blue Gum Camp?"

Zoe's mind raced. "In her present state, it's possible. She could remember how happy we all were there."

Jock nodded. "Go, then. I'll mind things here."

He seemed pleased to have a role to play, she thought, understanding how he felt. She only hoped she hadn't bitten off more than she could chew. On impulse she snatched up the mobile phone as well as the car keys from the study. The phone didn't always work in the shadow of the ranges, but anything was worth a try.

Struggling to remember everything James had shown her about handling the big vehicle, she aimed it in the direction of the bush camp, her eyes sweeping the underbrush as she drove.

Why hadn't she paid more attention to Genie's fears last night? She knew from her experience as a child-care worker that children's feelings often ran deep. Genie had already lost her mother. Now she faced the prospect of losing Zoe, too. It was more than a four-year-old should have to contemplate. What if it was too late? What if they didn't find her?

"Stop this," she ordered herself aloud. If anyone could find her, James would. This morning she glimpsed what loving him meant. It meant accepting that he was a man of action and wouldn't be stopped by her or anyone. Just as well they weren't really man and wife or she would have to live with this dread as a way of life. All the same, she knew she could find a way to bear it if only he loved her.

A disturbance in the underbrush shattered her thoughts and she slewed the car to a halt. But it was only a pretty-faced wallaby, its daytime rest disturbed by her passing. Doe-eyes flaring in panic, it bounded across the road and disappeared into the bush.

Heart pounding, she rested her head against the steering wheel until her breathing slowed. The sound of galloping hooves brought her head up again. This time it was a horse and she watched in horror as Amira, riderless, with stirrups and reins flying loose, reared out of the bush and tore down the track toward the homestead.

Alarm blistered through her. Where was the pony's young rider? Blindly, Zoe groped for the door handle and flung herself out of the car. "Genie? Genie, can you hear me? It's Mummy."

She was about to plunge into the bush in the direction from which the horse had come when another apparition rose in front of her. Instinctively she lifted her arms to shield her face, realizing belatedly that it was James astride Ferrere. She almost sagged with relief when she saw that he held Genie in the saddle in front of him.

"Oh thank God. Is she all right?"

"She's fine. A bit wet and bedraggled, but she'll be okay."

He didn't ask what she was doing out in the middle of the bush, but his stony expression told her the reckoning would come later. When she held up her arms, he handed the child down to her. Genie gave her a sheepish smile and linked her small arms around Zoe's neck. "Hi, Mummy. Amira took me for a ride."

"I'll say he did." Zoe's vision blurred as she smiled at the child, hugging her as if she would never let her go. "How did you manage to stop him?"

With economical movements James dismounted and dropped the reins over his horse's head. It immediately began to graze along the roadside. "She got off by sliding over Amira's head when the pony stopped to drink at a spring," he said.

The gruffness in his voice wasn't lost on Zoe. Nor was the fact that he looked worse than his daughter did. "Are you all right?" she asked in a low voice.

He gestured dismissively. "I'll live. More to the point, what are you doing here? I thought I told you to wait at the house."

At his sharp tone she bristled. "I felt I could be more useful out here. And before you yell at me, Jock's keeping an eye on things back at the homestead."

Genie looked up in alarm. "Are you going to yell at both of us, Daddy?"

His furious look swept them both. "I'm not yelling at anybody."

His tone belied his words. If not for Genie's presence,

he probably would yell at her, Zoe accepted. There wasn't much she could do right in his eyes. Loving him was probably her biggest crime, but she had no idea how to stop. Nor was she sure she wanted to, despite the pain that closed around her heart like a vise. She had thought she knew love when Genie came into her life, but it was only a foretaste of the passion she'd found with James. Knowing it couldn't last didn't stop her from thanking her stars for this brief glimpse of heaven.

She buried her face in Genie's damp sweater to hide her brimming eyes from him. "I'll drive you home in the car. You've had enough horse riding for one day, young lady."

Genie giggled. "I'm not a young lady yet. Is Daddy coming, too?"

Zoe was forced to meet his gaze. "Is he coming, too?"

He nodded. "I'll turn Ferrere into the paddock. He'll be fine until Grace comes for him." Having taken care of the horse, he slid into the passenger seat beside Zoe. Genie was bundled into a rug on the back seat and looked as if she might fall asleep before they reached the homestead.

She roused herself enough to ask, "Does this mean you won't go away now, Mummy?"

Zoe wanted to lock her eyes shut to avoid seeing James's face as he answered. What he said stunned her to her core. "Nobody's going away, sweetheart."

"Cross your heart?"

He gave Zoe a measured look. "Cross my heart."

How could he make such a promise, knowing it was bound to be broken? She couldn't ask in front of the little girl, so she fixed her eyes on the track ahead, glad of the steering wheel under her hands to give her shaking fingers something to latch on to.

As they neared the homestead James was able to contact Jock on the mobile phone. He promised to pass the good news to Grace and the other searchers as soon as they checked in. Genie was already a favorite with the staff so Zoe knew the news would travel around the property like wildfire.

She was right. Most of the stable staff found reasons to be on hand when James lifted Genie out of the car. Inside the homestead Grace had fresh coffee ready and hot chocolate for Genie. When the woman offered to bathe and change the little girl, Zoe started to resist until she felt James's restraining hand on her arm. "Let her. Genevieve will be all right," he insisted.

"You can't wait to separate me from her, can you?" Zoe asked tearfully as soon as Grace had taken the little girl upstairs.

He passed a hand across his eyes. "This has nothing to do with you. Grace blames herself for what happened and wants to make amends. She needs to know we still trust her with Genevieve."

She had to allow that he was right, Zoe thought, wishing she had realized what the other woman was going through. Trust James to put Grace's feelings before his own. Zoe didn't even want to think about how terrible he looked, as if he stayed on his feet by sheer willpower. He cradled a coffee mug in both hands and she noticed it shook slightly.

A red stain seeped through the dressing on his neck. "You're hurt," she said, horrified by how thin her voice sounded.

He touched the dressing and winced. "It's nothing. If you keep sounding like that, I'll think you actually care."

"You are my husband," she reminded him.

"In name only." Now who sounded as if he was starting to care? She tried to still the fast beating of her heart as he added, "It's the way you want it, isn't it?"

"Of course." She willed herself to sound as if she meant it. She noticed he hadn't said his feelings had changed. As long as all the love was on her side, nothing was going to change. But after his promise to Genie, she'd somehow hoped—

She drove the wish from her mind before it was fully formed. With Andrew she had experienced the pain of a one-sided love. She didn't intend to put herself through it again. James probably meant that he would allow her generous access to Genie. Zoe would have to be content with that.

He linked both hands behind his neck and dropped his head back. Her own concerns forgotten, she said at once, "You're in pain. I'm taking you to see Dr. Leigh."

James kept his eyes closed and a sheen of perspiration glistened on his face. "Howard isn't at home. Today he'll be at his surgery in Cooranbong."

"Then that's where we'll go," she said firmly. "You look terrible."

He gave her a wry look. "Thanks for the compliment. But the doc was right about the riding. My spine feels as if it's pushing up through my skull."

If he was *admitting* it—

She fetched the car keys and told Grace where they were going then kissed Genie and went down to find James waiting in the front seat of the car with his eyes shut and his head back. Cold fear clutched at her. "James?"

"I haven't passed out and I'm not planning to," he growled. "Let's get this over with."

His brusqueness had more to do with his pain than with her, she told herself firmly. The unmarked road was confusing and she had to keep a lookout for kangaroos crossing their path. In the end she slowed to a crawl, earning an ironic look from James. "I didn't break into pieces out there, Zoe."

She hadn't missed his indrawn breath every time she hit a bump, either. She stopped the car and wrenched the keys out of the ignition, dangling them in front of him. "Would you prefer to drive?"

He forced a weak grin. "Okay, message received. No more back-seat driving."

It was progress and she started the car again. Before she slid it into gear she looked across at him. "I know it's my fault that Genie ran away. I should have made sure she was out of earshot before I mentioned going away."

His jaw tightened perceptibly. "This is on my head as well. It's time I told her the truth and, more importantly, that we both love and want her. We'll tell her together tomorrow, so there's no need for you to blame yourself."

"I do blame myself and I don't want her loyalties divided between us anymore."

There was a moment of tense silence. "Are you trying to tell me you intend to go away for good?"

She nodded, fighting tears. "Genie…Genevieve is your child. She belongs here. She shouldn't be torn between the two people who love her." Her voice cracked but she forced herself to go on. "All I ask is that you let me know how she's doing. In time if I'm not around to remind her, she'll forget I was ever a part of her life."

"Is that what you want, Zoe?"

"It has to be. When I think what could have happened to her…" She bit down on the tears welling up again.

"What will you do?" he asked in an oddly clipped voice.

"Return to Sydney and try to rebuild my life. I might even meet someone and have a child of my own."

"Oh God, Zoe, don't." She had expected him to sound relieved. He had won, after all. But he sounded ground down.

It was probably his aggravated injury. She should probably have waited till he'd seen the doctor before raising the issue. But she was afraid if she postponed it her courage would fail her altogether.

Wearily she put the car into gear. "You might wish me happiness," she said.

This time there was no response.

She drove as carefully as she could, but he was still white to the eyes by the time they reached the doctor's surgery. Thankfully the waiting room was empty. Howard Leigh grunted when he saw James. "Crazy cowboy. Didn't I warn you to take things easy?"

Since James didn't seem inclined to, she explained about the search for Genie. The doctor led James into the surgery, muttering about "the indispensable man." But in this instance he was.

The warmth of the surgery lulled her into an exhausted doze. She awoke to find the doctor bending over her. "You look like you could use some attention yourself. Are you sure you're okay?"

She scrubbed her eyes. "I'm fine. How is James?"

He frowned. "About how you'd expect for a man who undid most of his surgeon's handiwork in one morning. I put in some new stitches and this time he must give them time to heal. You'll have to see to it that he does. He's getting dressed now."

She hesitated, wanting to go to James but unsure of her welcome. Then she squared her shoulders. This was, possibly, the last chance she would have. How could she *not* go to him?

In the surgery, she drank in the sight of him hungrily. As he shrugged on his shirt, he looked like an athlete in full training, the sculpted muscles of his chest emphasized by the checked fabric that hung open from his broad shoulders.

The doctor had replaced the dressing with a smaller one, but it was still a grim reminder of the risk James had taken. Relief at finding him on his feet surged through her and she sagged against the surgical table. "Oh, James, thank God you're all right."

He was beside her in an instant, supporting her with his good arm. His strength seemed to flow into her and she smiled shakily. "I should be the one helping you. When I think what could have happened..." She couldn't go on.

His arm tightened around her. "It didn't, so there's no need to look as if your world has come to an end."

"Are you sure it hasn't?"

His gaze impaled her. "Because of Genevieve?"

She could no longer choke back the betraying words which came out filtered by her tears. "Because of you. I know you don't want to hear it, but I love you, James. I won't let it get in your way, but..."

Whatever else she might have said was silenced by the force of his mouth crushing hers. Her senses swam, but it was so exactly where she wanted to be that she gladly surrendered to the feeling, putting into her kiss all the emotion she had been holding back for so long.

It came to her that she wasn't the only one, and she felt bewildered by the time he released her. "James?"

"You don't know how much I've wanted to hear you tell me you love me," he stated hoarsely. "Provided you meant it. Did you?"

She could only nod, her throat too choked for words.

It was enough. His breath rushed out. "All the time Howard was working on me, I was trying to work out how to convince you to stay. I can't let you go, Zoe. I love you too much."

"I don't understand," she said feeling dizzy. What had brought this miracle about?

His mouth tilted up playfully. "What part of 'I love you' don't you understand?"

"All of it. I thought you couldn't wait for me to leave."

Suddenly James seemed to shed much of his exhaustion.

He looked freshly overhauled and she hardly dared to believe it had something to do with the high-intensity look
he was directing at her. "I thought it was what you wanted.
Until you made me an offer that took the courage of a
lioness to make. Your offer to give me my daughter back
could only have been made out of love."

Fear rippled through her. "You're not saying this for
Genie's sake, are you?"

His lips roved over her eyes, mouth and throat. "This is
for my sake. I love you and I need you as my wife."

She was having trouble thinking straight. "But our
agreement—"

"You didn't read it, did you?"

"It was too long and technical so I just sighed it."

He gave a throaty chuckle. "As I hoped. It was simply
an insurance policy ensuring you get everything if anything
happened to me."

She stared at him wide-eyed, her pulse racing madly. His
kisses along the back of her neck didn't help her thinking
processes. "How did you intend to end our marriage without an official agreement?"

"The usual way—'till death do us part'."

Thinking of how close he had come twice, she sobered.
"When you didn't come around after the operation, and
again when you risked your recovery to find Genie today,
I thought I would lose you and I couldn't bear it."

"You weren't the only one," he admitted. "But until I
knew I had a future, it didn't seem fair to tell you. Then
afterward I wasn't sure you wanted to hear it."

"I told you I loved you after the operation."

He smiled lazily. "So I didn't imagine what you said."

She felt a blush starting. "You weren't supposed to hear
that."

"Thank goodness I did. Your love was what pulled me

back from the brink. You nearly told me tonight, before I went to look for Genevieve, didn't you?"

So he had guessed after all. Joy shrilled through her. "I will always love you, James."

At the surgery door, the doctor gave a discreet cough. "There's a good hotel across the road, you two."

James grinned but didn't loosen his hold on her. "Is that your medical opinion, Howard?"

"Sure is. My prescription is for bed rest and lots of warmth."

James looked down at her. "You heard the doctor. Do you think Grace would mind keeping an eye on Genevieve—Genie—for one more night?"

His use of the nickname thrilled her. But his proposal thrilled her more. "They were having fun when I left, so I don't think she'll mind." Zoe knew she certainly didn't.

The bed and the warmth were easily provided by the local hotel, but she had a feeling it would be a long time before they got to the resting part. "Dr. Leigh is a smart man," she murmured as she snuggled close to James much, much later. "He seems to know all about the healing power of love."

James's mouth moved over hers in a lingering kiss that tasted of the future. Their future together. "So do I, my darling. This is my prescription exactly."

She raised an eyebrow at him. "Howard might have something to say about you practicing medicine without a license."

His eyes sparkled with the brilliance of love. "May I remind you, Mrs. Langford, we do have a license for what we're practicing—a marriage license."

"But it wasn't meant to be real," she said, still bemused by the transformation in their relationship. James was truly her husband, to have and to hold from this day forward. Genie was really her child, the first of the family James had promised her as he whispered sweet words of love into her ear.

"I'll show you how real it is," he vowed, taking her into his arms. Dawn was painting the sky with gold by the time she admitted to being completely convinced.

Epilogue

Would she ever get used to seeing her child astride one of James's powerful Arabian horses? Zoe asked herself. Her nerves were in shreds by the time Genie's mount cleared the first of the jumps, tackled by her rider with gentle hands and a skillful touch. Zoe choked back her fear as Genie set her horse at a wall higher than any she had jumped before.

Fearless and magnificent, Genie spurred the spirited horse forward. Together they cleared the jump in perfect harmony, landing safely on the far side. Zoe decided it was safe to breathe again.

"Our daughter's come a long way, hasn't she?" James murmured into her ear.

She reached for his hand, her throat filling. Not so long ago she'd despaired of hearing Genie described in those words. And most of all of having the love of the man at her side. "So have we," she agreed.

She sneaked a look at him. His sheer physical presence still thrilled her, especially when she saw his effect on other people. The strength in him, the set of his jaw, and the wide shoulders all bespoke a masculinity to be reckoned with. When he smiled at her as he did now, the sheer brilliance of it still possessed the power to snatch her breath away.

How did I get to be so lucky? she wondered as her gaze took in her men around her, James on her right, and four-year-old Jimmy on her left. Her heart filled to overflowing as she gathered her husband and son in her outstretched arms.

The gymkhana was over and the stirring strains of the national anthem brought them to their feet. As Genie stepped forward to receive her prize, Zoe clung to James, her heart swelling to a bursting point. Their daughter grew more like her father every day and, thankfully, had his generosity of spirit. Genie had readily accepted James's explanation about why she had been taken away from him. His unrelenting efforts to find her had shown her how much he cared. It had forged a remarkable bond between father and daughter, which grew stronger as the years passed.

Like the bond between herself and James, Zoe thought dreamily. When she first confessed her love to him, she had never suspected that it could actually increase the longer they were together, until it became their haven in the good times and their shield against the bad. Nothing would ever come between them, she knew with unshakable certainty. Unquenchable and eternal, theirs was a love to last for all time.

* * * * *

Welcome to the Towers!

In January
New York Times bestselling author

NORA ROBERTS

takes us to the fabulous Maine coast mansion
haunted by a generations-old secret and introduces
us to the fascinating family that lives there.

Mechanic Catherine "C.C." Calhoun and hotel magnate
Trenton St. James mix like axle grease and mineral
water—until they kiss. Efficient Amanda Calhoun finds
easygoing Sloan O'Riley insufferable—and irresistible.
And they all must race to solve the mystery
surrounding a priceless hidden emerald necklace.

Catherine and Amanda

THE Calhoun Women

A special 2-in-1 edition containing
COURTING CATHERINE and A MAN FOR AMANDA.

Look for the next installment of
THE CALHOUN WOMEN with Lilah and Suzanna's
stories, coming in March 1998.

Available at your favorite retail outlet.

He's more than a man, he's one of our

Join Silhouette Romance as we present these heartwarming tales about wonderful men facing the challenges of fatherhood and love.

January 1998:

THE BILLIONAIRE'S BABY CHASE by Valerie Parv (SR#1270)
Billionaire daddy James Langford finds himself falling for Zoe Holden, the alluring foster mother of his long-lost daughter.

March 1998:

IN CARE OF THE SHERIFF by Susan Meier (SR#1283)
Sexy sheriff Ryan Kelly becomes a father-in-training when he is stranded with beautiful Madison Delaney and her adorable baby.

May 1998:

FALLING FOR A FATHER OF FOUR by Arlene James (SR#1295)
Overwhelmed single father Orren Ellis is soon humming the wedding march after hiring new nanny Mattie Kincaid.

Fall in love with our FABULOUS FATHERS!

And be sure to look for additional FABULOUS FATHERS titles in the months to come.

Available at your favorite retail outlet.

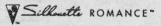 ROMANCE™

Look us up on-line at: http://www.romance.net   SRFFJ-M

FIVE STARS
MEAN SUCCESS

If you see the "5 Star Club" flash on a book,
it means we're introducing you to one of our
most STELLAR authors!

Every one of our Harlequin and Silhouette
authors who has sold over 5 MILLION BOOKS
has been selected for our "5 Star Club."

We've created the club so you won't miss
any of our bestsellers. So, each month
we'll be highlighting every original book within
Harlequin and Silhouette written by our
bestselling authors.

NOW THERE'S NO WAY ON EARTH OUR
STARS WON'T BE SEEN!

5 STAR CLUB
AUTHOR

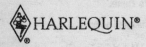 HARLEQUIN®   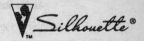 Silhouette®

Our *5 Star Club* authors are successful authors who have sold **over 5 million books**. In honor of their success, we're offering you a <u>**FREE**</u> gift and a chance to look like a million bucks!

You can choose:

the necklace...

the bracelet...

or the earrings...

Or indulge, and receive all three!

To receive one item, send in 1 (one)* proof of purchase, plus $1.65 U.S./$2.25 CAN. for postage and handling, to:

In the U.S.
Harlequin 5 Star Club
3010 Walden Ave.
P.O. Box 9047
Buffalo, NY
14269-9047

In Canada
Harlequin 5 Star Club
P.O. Box 636
Fort Erie, Ontario
L2A 5X3

* To receive more than one piece of jewelry, send in another proof of purchase and an additional 25¢ for each extra item.

**5 STAR CLUB—
PROOF OF PURCHASE**

Inventory:	Item:	
721-1	Necklace	❑
722-9	Bracelet	❑
723-7	Earrings	❑

Name: _____

Address: _____

City: _____

State/Prov.: _____ Zip/Postal Code: _____

Account number:_____ (if applicable)

093 KGI CFKZ   *Silhouette®*

093 KGI CFKZ

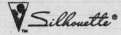